LOVED BY THE VISCOUNT

HAPPILY EVER AFTER BOOK 5

ELLIE ST. CLAIR

Facebook: Ellie St. Clair

Cover by AJF Designs

Do you love historical romance? Receive access to a free ebook, as well as exclusive content such as giveaways, contests, freebies and advance notice of pre-orders through my mailing list!

Sign up here!

Also By Ellie St. Clair

Standalone
Unmasking a Duke

Happily Ever After
The Duke She Wished For
Someday Her Duke Will Come
Once Upon a Duke's Dream
He's a Duke, But I Love Him
Loved by the Viscount

Searching Hearts
Quest of Honor
Clue of Affection

Hearts of Trust
Hope of Romance

CONTENTS

THE DUKE SHE WISHED FOR

QUEST OF HONOR

1

The cemetery was silent but for the call of a bird in the distance.

Rosalind heard footsteps approaching from behind her, but she didn't turn to look as she continued to stare out over the small plot of headstones in front of her.

Her husband was dead. Lord Harold Branson, Earl of Templeton, had fallen down the stairs of a brothel in a drunken stupor. When he hit the landing at the bottom, his head had cracked against the floor so hard that he had broken his neck.

"Rosalind," came a soft voice behind her, and she felt Olivia's cool hand on her arm. She turned around and looked up at her friend, whose face was wreathed in concern. "Are you quite all right?

The former Lady Rosalind Kennedy, made Lady Templeton but months ago, murmured a simple yes and nodded at Olivia. For what else was there to say?

The spring day was warm, and the sun shone brightly over the acres of grass stretching out in front of her, so at odds with the darkness that had invaded her soul. She wasn't supposed to be out here; rather, she was to be in seclusion to mourn the man who had given her his name and his home and yet had taken so much away from her.

Only a few had seen the man actually buried, of course, but she had to see for herself that he was truly gone, see the fresh mound of dirt piled over his grave. Thankfully, the fact she was so newly and apparently so deeply in mourning meant that she did not have to maintain the facade of polite hostess in receiving those who had gathered here at their country home. She hardly knew what to say to them. It was one thing if one's husband had died from sickness or in battle. It was quite another when he had practically fallen out of the arms of a prostitute to his death.

And so she had affixed a smile to her face and routinely repeated the same words over and over to any she met, thanking them for their kindness in her hour of need. Thank goodness Harold's mother was no longer alive to know of her son's actions. Unfortunately, his father had been just the same. It was difficult enough to have her own parents looking at her as they did, her mother with some pity, her father with disdain.

"I do not want to go back inside," she whispered, cursing her trembling lips. With Olivia, her longest friend, she could be honest and share her true thoughts and feelings.

"I know, darling," Olivia said, putting her arm around her and pulling her in close. "I wouldn't either. But rest assured, all will soon be gone. It is rather odd there are so many people here, but it seems your brother-in-law was eager for all to see him as the newly appointed earl."

Rosalind nodded in understanding, blinking back the tear beginning to leak out of her eye.

Olivia misinterpreted it.

"I am sorry, Ros," she said. "I know how much you must

miss Harold, despite what happened. And I am sorry that he ... was where he was at the time of his death. I'm not entirely sure what is truth and what is gossip, but you must know that you are welcome to speak to me about it, anytime you wish."

Rosalind turned her vacant stare back to Olivia, feeling her heart harden. She had not told Olivia of what her marriage to Harold had been like, had not wanted to feel her pity. Olivia wanted to solve any problem she came across, but there was nothing she could have done regarding Rosalind's situation. Now, however, it no longer mattered.

"I do not miss him," she said with so much vehemence that Olivia jumped a bit in surprise.

"That's understandable too," her friend said in a conciliatory tone.

"No, you do not understand," Rosalind repeated, looking around to make sure they were truly alone. "I am *glad* that he is gone. I am *happy* he is dead. I hated him, Olivia, and now that he is gone, I feel free."

Olivia's mouth formed a round O as she took in her words, and Rosalind could see that she had shocked the normally unflappable Olivia Finchley, Duchess of Breckenridge.

"Well," she finally managed, and Rosalind saw the corners of her mouth tugging up slightly. "I must say, Rosalind, I am proud of you!"

"Proud?"

"Why, yes," she said. "For once in your life, you are allowing yourself to feel how you *want* to feel, not how you think you ought to."

Rosalind sighed. "Oh, Olivia, does not thinking so make me the most horrible person you've ever met? How can one be glad upon the death of another, especially one's husband?"

"A woman has every right to be glad, particularly if her husband was an absolute boor," said Olivia, crossing her arms. "I never liked Harold, anyway."

Rosalind was shocked at Olivia's words. She had always acted pleasant enough to Harold. "Why did you never say so?"

Olivia shrugged. "I thought you loved him."

"I loved the idea of him," Rosalind said, beginning to lead Olivia back to the house, as much as she would have preferred to stay out here — even in the cemetery — until everyone departed. "I loved the idea of being married. And it was what my parents thought best. He was always kind and considerate while we courting. Once we married, he was nice enough, if slightly disconnected. And then after only a few weeks, he became rather mean and obnoxious. My feelings, my thoughts, mattered naught. He called me his, 'pathetic little wife,' and spoke to me only if it were an order or an insult. Oh Olivia, I could hardly stand him! And then when he died..."

Rosalind recalled being informed of her husband's death. They were in London, as her husband found the country far too tedious and had loved going out to his gentlemen's clubs. One of his friends had come to the door in the middle of the night, and her maid had woken her. Rosalind had put on her wrapper and met the man in the drawing room, where he ground out the words to her, his face tight as she pushed to know the details of what had happened. She gave the man credit, however, as he hadn't held back, but had told her all she had wanted to know.

She had sat there, unmoving, unspeaking, unsure what to think of the news as her emotions tumbled inside her.

Finally she had reverted back to how she had been raised — to respond to any revelation with a cool politeness, not showing any emotion. She had thanked the man, who left rather hastily although not without a backward look of concern, and she had returned to her room, where she lay in bed, unable to sleep, for the rest of the night.

"There is nothing of which you should be ashamed," said Olivia firmly, drawing her back to the present. "However, I do wish you had told me of your feelings. You are always so stoic, so unflappable, that is hard to read what you are thinking."

"It is better that way," Rosalind said. She knew her mother had always wanted what was best for her, and yet had been so critical, so demanding, that Rosalind had learned to hide her thoughts and feelings from the world for fear of judgment.

"I do know, however, that I can trust you, Olivia, and I appreciate that more than you know."

Rosalind smiled at her friend. "And now, only one more wretched afternoon with all of these people, and then I shall be free to do as I please. I know I will not have access to the same funds as when Harold was alive, but my small stipend is all I shall need to live out the rest of my days happily. Perhaps I will find a small cottage somewhere, or a townhouse in London."

She stared away at the hills dreamily, picturing a quiet existence where she could read and write and take in all of the dogs and the cats she could ever want. Harold had refused when she had told him she wanted her own little dog for company. She no longer had to worry about that. She would, however, miss the opportunity to have children. If there was one thing she had longed for in life, it was to be a mother, but sadly it seemed not to be.

"In time, you will likely marry again," said Olivia gently, but Rosalind shook her adamantly.

"No," she said. "I no longer trust who a man may become. I thought Harold a good sort, and look how wrong I was! One never knows what one may get. You were lucky with Alastair; however, there is no guarantee that would be so for me."

Olivia gave her a sad smile but said nothing, seemingly content to link arms with her and walk back to the house in companionship.

William Elliot, Viscount of Southam, looked out the window of Lord Harold Branson's drawing room at the two figures drawing near the house. Well, he supposed it wasn't Lord Harold's any longer, but his brother Bartholomew's. The man seemed to already have made himself comfortable in his new role of earl, a wide smile on his face as he welcomed guests into his home but days after the death of his brother.

Alastair Finchley, Duke of Breckenridge, came to stand beside him and joined him in peering out at his wife and the small figure next to her. William looked over at the man with a nod. They were not exactly friends as they hadn't gotten off to the greatest beginning, but they had grown to be respectful of one another.

In truth, there was no reason to hold out any animosity toward Breckenridge. It wasn't his fault that William had been in love with his wife since childhood.

The lovely, intriguing, unique Lady Olivia, however, had never seen him as anything other than one of her best friends, perhaps a brother more than anything. They had grown up together, their families' country estates being so close. He had always been there for her, through one scheme after another as she found herself in all sorts of trouble, usually of her own making. Even this past year, he was there by her side as she fell deeper in love with the duke who now stood beside him.

"'Tis a sad day for Lady Rosalind," Alastair said now, breaking the silence. "She was not only left a widow but humiliated by her husband, even in death. Olivia never liked the man."

"No," agreed William. "He was certainly something of a cur from what I knew of him, although fortunately we did not run in the same circles. I am not sure what shall become of her."

"She will live off some the income of the estate for a time, and she will have part of her dowry to sustain her. More than likely she will marry again."

William wasn't as certain. He had never been particularly close with Rosalind, as she had always been a somewhat quiet, timid thing. She had been friends with Olivia since childhood, and whenever the Kennedys came to visit, they would spend time together. Rosalind had never said much to him, though she would watch him with those wide eyes and hesitantly follow him and Olivia from one scheme to the next. She let Olivia do the talking for her, preferring to spend her time with a book or in the barn playing with the kittens. She was a pretty thing but always seemed to be outshined by the brightness of her friend.

He could see, however, that it would be rather hard for anyone to stand out next to Olivia. He knew Olivia's mother had always despaired of her and her outlandish schemes, but William was always there, her "Billy" by her side, taking the blame along with her. He would do anything for her. He sighed now, looking out at her blonde head next to Rosalind's dark one. He would have married Olivia, but she had always been determined to find love, and clearly she had not found that in him. Nor would her mother have ever wanted her daughter to marry a simple viscount.

"Do you know her well?"

It took a moment for William to realize the Duke was speaking of Rosalind, and not his own wife.

"Ah, somewhat," he replied. "We met now and again as children, but she has always been a quiet sort. I have made her acquaintance in London at the odd social gathering, but that is all."

"She is a gentle soul, is she not?"

"I suppose that is the best way to describe her," William responded with a shrug. "I do not wish to speak ill of the dead, but hopefully in due time she will realize she is better off without her husband."

"One can only hope," the Duke replied, and as they parted ways, William realized that for once his gaze had lingered not on the woman he had thought he had loved for so long, but rather on the small figure dwarfed in black. As she held her head high and wore a drawn yet resolute look, he felt a pull to help her out of her current situation, although he knew it was not his place.

Ah well, he thought, turning from the window. She had her family and her friends. Her problems were none of his concern.

2

Rosalind saw all eyes turn toward her as she entered the drawing room. They were so filled with pity that she did not want, and she longed to run from them all to her bedroom and hide under the covers for the rest of the day. Thankfully she *could* do so, but, alas, not immediately. No, Rosalind did as she always did — what was expected of her. She walked around the guests, thanking them for coming and making the polite conversation she so hated.

She began to make her way over to Olivia when her arm was caught in a tight grasp, and she turned to find Harold's brother Bart in her face. Oh, how she hated him. She had always felt his lecherous gaze on her, which he made even less attempt to hide now that Harold was gone.

"If you have a moment, Rosalind, I must speak with you — alone," he said, a somewhat sinister smile crossing his face and making her shiver.

"Now?" she asked, looking around the room. "Do you not think perhaps we should wait until you have finished entertaining your guests?"

"*Our* guests, my dear," he said with a condescending look. "I think now is best. Come."

Rosalind didn't want to follow him, but she wanted to make a scene even less, and so she decided the least amount of conflict could be found by getting through this conversation as quickly as possible.

Rather than allowing her to enter the room first, Bart brushed past her into the study that had been her husband's. It was dark, the walls a deep navy blue that seemed to cave in on her, and as she sat in the hard, straight-back leather chair in front of the desk, she nervously twisted her hands in her lap while Bart looked down at her, his lips twisted in a malicious grin that reminded her of a hunter who had trapped his prey and meant to toy with it.

"Rosalind," he said with relish as he stood, rounded the desk, and sat on the edge of it just inches from her. She tried to flinch away from his nearness, as her entire body loathed to even be in the same room as him. "I am sorry about my brother's passing," he said, reaching out a finger to tip her chin up toward him, sending a shudder down her spine.

"Yes, you have said that," she said, jerking her head back.

"There is more, however," he continued, his mouth stretching to show his crooked, uneven teeth, and when he realized just how uncomfortable she was by his presence, he leaned toward her even more. "My brother, unfortunately, did not see to your settlement."

"My settlement?" she echoed, confused by his words. "You mean to live off of after his passing?"

"Exactly."

"I am unsure of what the issue would be. I know I have money that would have been set aside from my dowry," she said, trying to ignore the increased speed of her heart fluttering in her chest. "I am not sure exactly how much there is, but it should be more than enough. My father was very generous."

"Yes, well, there was money there, but unfortunately, my brother had a few vices, as you well know, and there is nothing left."

Rosalind's jaw dropped open as she watched him finally push back from the desk and resume his seat behind it.

"That's impossible," she said, trying not to let the sudden panic seep into her voice. "There was always money, for my wardrobe, for the staff, for the house — why, there was even money for the funeral! Besides that, I am entitled, by law mind you, to one-third of the estate's profits, and *that* you cannot—" she stopped as he raised a hand, cutting her off.

"What money remains is tied up with the title," he said, beginning to organize papers on the desk as if their conversation held little importance. "While you were married to my brother, the estate made nothing, but rather in actuality lost money. You could receive profits, it's true, but there are none. In fact, I will be repaying debts for many a day. There is nothing left for you."

"But—"

"Fortunately, I have a solution."

She narrowed her eyes. Whatever he had in mind, she knew, would not be agreeable. He stopped shuffling papers and looked at her.

"You shall marry me, and I will provide you with everything you had with my brother."

He sat back in the leather chair and steepled his fingers in front of him, looking particularly pleased by his own words.

She shot up from her chair, not caring that her shock and disgust was likely evident on her face. "I will never," she ground out. "How could you think that I would even consider such a thing?"

"Now Rosalind," he said, leaning forward. "I know that you may not particularly care for me, but with time I'm sure we can come to an amiable relationship."

"Not care for you?" she said, her anger flaring, so unlike her except in moments such as this, when all was at stake. "I abhor you! You seduce young girls, you frequent more brothels than Harold did, and you even propositioned me while I was still married to your brother! I will never marry you. Never."

"I know you may be grieving my brother, and I understand that. Luckily for you, I am a kind man," he chuckled as if he had heard nothing she had said. "I will give you your year of mourning, although primarily to make sure that should you birth any little creatures, we know exactly whose they may be. You will live here with me or in the London house. The choice is yours. But in a year's time, we shall marry and continue with our lives – together."

He raised his eyebrows at her, seemingly satisfied she would fall in line with his plan, and she was well aware of what it might be like to be married to such a man. Harold was bad enough. Bart would be even worse. No, she would not allow it to be.

"Thank you for your offer," she choked the words out. "I am flattered. However, I believe I shall, instead, return to my parents. If you will excuse me."

She strode to the door angrily as she heard him laugh behind her. "Good luck," he said. "I believe you will find your father, however, is already in agreement with me. He seemed quite amenable to the idea."

Rosalind refused to turn and acknowledge his words, though she felt her limbs beginning to shake in fear and uncertainty. His words scared her, for she knew that if Bart had spoken to them, in all likelihood her parents had agreed. They cared for her, true, but they cared more to have seen her married into a good family. Her marriage to Harold was proof enough of that.

She flung open the door, startled to find her parents waiting just down the corridor from the room she had exited. They must have known this conversation was taking place.

"Mother, Father," she said, rushing up to them in a manner she knew her mother would deem rather unladylike. "Please tell me what he said is not true. What do you know of this?"

Her mother looked rather apologetic, but they both seemed rather resolute. Her father sighed as he looked at her. "Unfortunately, it has recently come to my attention that your late husband squandered away your dowry and left nothing for you. What Templeton — this Templeton — says is correct. Everything else is tied up with the title. It would be best if you marry him as he wishes."

"No," she said, shaking her head in shock. "Have you met the man? He is horrific. I cannot marry him. I *will* not. Can I not come live with you, at least until I determine my next steps?"

"It took some time to find a suitable match for you to begin with," her father said, and Rosalind recognized the tight set to his face that told her he did not want to be argued with. "Your brother will be of age soon and will be in search of a wife. It would be easier for him to not have his widowed sister to look after. Therefore, Rosalind, it would be much simpler were you to simply marry Templeton now. In fact, daughter, I will *not* be questioned on this."

"Father, you cannot be serious!" she said, backing up a

step in disbelief. "Harold was bad enough, but at least, for the most part, he simply left me alone for the few months we were married."

"Yes," her mother said, "and that was the problem, Rosalind. You did not keep your husband interested enough, and so he went elsewhere, and he died because of it. Your name will now be something of a laughingstock in society and it will be difficult for you to marry again, which you must in order to survive. This time around, you must do better, Rosalind. I raised you to know how to keep a man interested."

Rosalind blinked, hardly believing that her parents could be so cruel. They had never been exactly warm, and yet this was unheard of. Her husband was — quite literally — in the ground for not even an hour, and her parents and brother-in-law were already scheming against her.

She couldn't look at them any longer, and she pushed away from the doorway, hurrying through the corridor to the library, the room that had been her solace these past months. She shut the door behind her and stumbled to the leather chesterfield, which she collapsed down upon.

Unbidden, tears began to form, and she willed them back. She would not cry, she told herself. She had not cried when she heard of her husband's death. She had not cried when she watched through the window as they had buried him in the ground. But now, all of the anger and frustration began to build and came spilling out of her eyes, and she let her head fall into her hands and wept.

She wasn't sure how long she let the tears fall, allowing herself this moment of self-pity, but once her tears began to dry she sniffed loudly, searching for a handkerchief as silence filled the room.

She would not go back out there, she told herself. No.

For once in her life, she was going to do what she wanted to do, and that was return to her chamber and speak to no one else for the remainder of this day.

She stood and was wiping at her face with her sleeve when she heard a creak. Her head snapped up, and she looked around the room. "Hello?" She called, feeling a tingle down her back. Suddenly she was aware of a presence in the room and took tentative steps toward the rows of bookshelves. "Is someone there?"

Footsteps finally came hesitantly around the corner, and stepping out from behind one of the shelves was William Elliot, who was now, she had been told, the Viscount of Southam.

She swallowed. Why, out of everyone present at this blasted reception, was it him, standing now in front of her? As children, she had always had a bit of a penchant for him, and she gathered he knew it as well. He had grown into a man who was fine and worthy indeed. He was what she would have wanted in a husband. He was good-looking, yes, but he was also kind, generous, and had a lovely sense of humor. He knew how to make people feel at ease, and gentlemen welcomed him to social outings while women loved to flirt with him. She had always known, however, that he had eyes for no one but Olivia.

Even so, anytime she was in his presence she seemed to stumble over her words, her attraction to him like a fence, obstructing any words that wanted to come out of her mouth. And now here he was, witnessing her blubbering like an idiot.

She simply stood and stared at him for a moment. She opened her mouth to speak, but all she could think of was the fact she must look like a fish, as all words escaped her.

~

WILLIAM FELT LIKE SUCH A LOUT. He had come to the library in search of a good brandy, for what Templeton was serving was not worth giving to swine. He had been searching the sideboard when he heard Lady Templeton arrive. He was going to announce himself when he had heard her tears begin, and he had slunk back into the shadows. He had hoped to wait until she left so that she would never know he had been there.

Clearly she had been searching for a moment alone to grieve, and he had unintentionally completely intruded. His legs had become cramped, however, and as he tried to find a new position, he had made enough noise to alert her to his presence. He now stood in front of her like a child caught sticking his fingers in the pudding.

"Lord Southam," she finally said, twining her fingers together in embarrassment as she realized he had witnessed her entire episode on the chesterfield. Her cheeks turned a bright pink, matching her red-rimmed eyes and nose. He winced as he could tell she was clearly not pleased to see him. "What are you—"

"I must apologize," he said hastily. "I came in here in search of good brandy. When you entered, I was going to say something, but then, well..." he didn't know what to say to improve the situation.

"You will certainly not find any good brandy remaining in this house," she said with a sad smile which quickly faded. "I am sorry you had to see that," she added quietly, looking down. The black she wore rather dwarfed her small frame, and he knew that a woman with her coloring — her dark hair and pale skin — would look much better in pastels or vibrant colors. He hoped, for her sake, it wouldn't be long until she returned to them. A strange sensation had come over him, making him long to take her in his arms and comfort her, to tell her all would be all right. He suppressed the feeling as quickly as it had arisen. She was just made a widow, for goodness sake.

"Not at all," he said softly. "I can understand how you must miss your husband. I am sorry that you had such a short time together."

"Oh," she said with a bit of a start. "No, it is not that at all. Rather—"

She was interrupted when there came a soft knock at the door.

"Ros, are you in there?"

Olivia must have come looking for her friend, William realized. With a nod from Rosalind — having known her as a girl, he really couldn't think of her as Lady Templeton, he realized — he strode over and opened the door, Olivia spilling in.

"Rosalind, what — oh Billy, what are you doing here?" She looked at him quizzically.

"I am just taking my leave," he said, relieved that Olivia was now here to comfort Rosalind. He certainly wasn't any help and had rather made the entire situation worse. "I must leave at first light, and so should be soon to bed. Goodnight, Olivia, Lady Templeton."

"Rosalind," came the reply, so soft he almost didn't hear it.

"Pardon me?"

"Do not call me Lady Templeton, please," she said, and he didn't know what to make of the bite he heard in her tone. "Call me Rosalind instead."

"All right then, Lady Rosalind," he said, confused, but

then who was he to argue with a grieving woman? "Again, my condolences. Farewell."

And with that, he stepped out of the library, away from the distressed lady and the woman he loved, doing his best to remove both of them from his thoughts.

3

ne year later

"I'M IN TROUBLE, BILLY."

William Elliot, Viscount of Southam, sighed as his brother walked into the room and sat down in the straight back chair in front of his desk. This wasn't exactly a revelation. His brother Alfred was always in trouble.

"What did you do now, Alf?" he asked as he reached down to scratch his mongrel canine, Friday, between the ears.

"I didn't do anything," his brother said, resting his chin on his fist as he leaned on William's desk. Of course he didn't do anything, thought William. Alfred was always quick to find someone else to blame. "You see, I met this man at a club, and he was telling me all about his business. It was rather fascinating. All about... Anyway, he said he knew this investment could make quite a lot of money, and he only needed a bit of support, if you will, to get it running."

"You gave him money, didn't you Alf." William stated rather than questioned, knowing the truth. He rubbed at his forehead, feeling a bit of a headache beginning to form. They came on often and suddenly, particularly when his brother came to see him.

"How did you know?" his brother looked shocked. Alfred was many things, thought William, but he wasn't very swift.

"Because you always throw your money away on one scheme or another," said William. "When are you ever going to learn?"

"Well, we cannot all become titled viscounts," said Alfred with some contempt, raking his hand through his tawny brown hair, so like William's own. In fact, they looked almost like twins, and yet they were as different as two brothers could be who had been raised in the same household. Alfred was much like their mother, while William took after their late father, a man he had idolized and still greatly missed.

"You are telling me you would want my responsibility?" William asked somewhat incredulously. "I should hardly think this would be the life you would choose, Alf."

Alfred sat back mulishly. "Perhaps not. However, I am going to need an increase in my yearly allowance."

"How much?"

"You'll need to double it," he said with a shrug, as if it was a casual sum.

"Double it?" William was aghast. His brother had never been too proud to ask for more than was due to him, but this was more than a bit much. "Alfred, you act as if Father left a fortune behind, which you know is far from the case.

You are the second son of a viscount, and as unfair as you feel that may be, at some point you are going to have to make money for yourself through a respectable profession, not through these schemes where you are simply throwing away money."

"Just this one time, Billy," Alfred said, trying to placate him with an affable grin.

William stared at his brother. He wasn't sure what to do with him anymore. His father had always been rather too lenient, allowing him to do whatever he pleased, and while William would be fine with Alfred going about and doing as he wished, what he had issue with was Alfred continuing to come back to him for help. He was done with it.

"No," he said resolutely, coming to his feet to signal the conversation was at an end. "You will have to find your own way out of this one, Alf. I can no longer bail you out. Time and time again you come to me to solve your problems, and it's at an end."

"But Bill—"

"You can live here or at our London home if you wish," said William, sweeping his hands out to signify their modest country estate. "The doors will always be open to you, and your basic needs will be met. However, I will no longer fund your escapades or your disastrous ideas. You shall have to determine how to fund your lifestyle yourself, or you may simply have to stay away from your vices and be responsible. And do not go asking Mother for help."

Alfred's mouth dropped open in astonishment, as if he could hardly believe someone was saying no to him. But William was resolute. It was the right thing to do, or else he would spend the rest of his life funding Alfred's next scheme.

"Fine then," Alfred said, a look of anger now distorting

his features as he stood. "If that is what you wish, then so be it."

As he stormed out of the room, William sat back down at his desk, massaging his temples as the headache hit him with full force.

HER ONE YEAR WAS UP.

Rosalind had thought a year would be long enough to determine what next to do. She had considered her options. She had originally thought she would become a governess. She was intelligent enough, and she loved to read and write. However, the issue was that she wasn't particularly good at sharing that intelligence with others. She had actually found herself a two-week stint with one family. She had loved the children, but they weren't particularly well behaved and refused to listen to anything she had to say. She had left in frustration, thinking that perhaps she would be better working as an upper servant.

She had tried to find work, but when they found out she was the widow of an earl, they had laughed in her face. Why would they hire a noblewoman, who would clearly lack the skills they sought? No, they felt she would think herself, be much too highbred, unable to follow orders, and assumed she would likely leave within a fortnight.

What Rosalind *had* done well was avoid Bart. He was primarily in London, so she spent much of her time at the country estate. The servants were sympathetic toward her, and when they heard any rumor that he was coming to visit, they would warn her and she would leave before he arrived, likely unknowingly crossing paths with him on the road as she made her way to London, or traveled to stay with friends.

The year of mourning was rather ridiculous, she thought, given that she had only been married to Harold but three months. Nevertheless, she was grateful as it was a year of reprieve from Bart and her parents.

Now, she looked down at the piece of paper held in her hands, the words scratched in Bart's scribbled, terrible penmanship.

Rosalind, my dear. The time has come for us to be married. I look forward to seeing you within a sennight and will bid your parents to join us to celebrate.

That would never happen, she vowed. She had done what was asked of her throughout her entire life, and look where that had gotten her — marriage to Harold Branson.

Only one person could allow her to be happy — herself. And happiness certainly wouldn't be found in a life with Bart Branson. No, she had learned from her experiences and she knew now what she needed to do. She had to forge a new identity for herself, and then find work. It would be a different life than she had always known, but she was determined to see it through. In the meantime, however, she needed somewhere to stay, and she decided she would make her way to the country estate Olivia shared with her husband, the Duke of Breckenridge, and create her new life for herself.

The servants here at the Templeton estate were all tied to the home, and she could not even bring her lady's maid with her, as she would have no means of paying the girl. She could have a loyal groom accompany her to Olivia's home, but from there, she was on her own.

At least, she thought as she began to pack one small bag to take with her, she could now dispense with the dreary black. She was entirely sick of it. She knew she should now only wear half-mourning clothes of gray and lavender, but if she were to become a new woman, did it really matter? She decided to pack one of each color in case they were needed in social circumstances in the near future, in addition to her favorite dresses, which she hadn't worn in so long now they were likely out of fashion.

No matter, she thought with a shrug and dragged the now heavy bag down the stairs.

"Are you certain you don't want to take one of the maids as a companion, my lady?" The groom questioned her for the third time since she had told him of the travel plans yesterday, and Rosalind tried not to show her exasperation.

"Yes, James," she said, as he helped her with the bag. "I will be fine."

"And this is all you are taking?"

"It is," she said with a nod, and he finally seemed resigned. The Breckenridge estate was less than a day's journey, and Rosalind told James he would be able to stay the night and then return the next day.

For an estate that was apparently destitute, the carriage was rather ostentatious, thought Rosalind. But that was just like the Branson family — as long as others thought them to be wealthy, that was all that really mattered.

She closed her eyes and leaned her head back against the squabs as they trundled down the lane. One last carriage ride in luxury, she thought, so she might as well enjoy it. She wished she could take out a book and pass the journey in the blessed company of a story to take her mind off her own life, but alas, the motion of the carriage always made her stomach tangle in knots, and reading made it all the worse. Instead, she would have to sit here with her own thoughts.

Her mind went back to her short marriage with Harold. She had known, the moment she stood on that altar, that she should not have been marrying him. Yet she was so averse to conflict, to causing a scene, that she went along with it. *How stupid, to ruin your entire life's happiness because you didn't want people to see you in a bad light,* she thought to herself, her face tightening in shame. And yet, that was who she had always been — Rosalind the peacemaker, doing what everyone else wanted, what everyone thought best — except herself.

She pressed cool fingers to her eyes, thinking back over the last year and a half of her life. For the first month of her marriage, Harold had been the man he always had been — not particularly warm, no, but kind enough, allowing her to do as she wished. Then, slowly, he had changed. She couldn't say there was a moment when he had become someone else, but rather it had happened gradually. One day he might forbid her from accepting an invitation to visit a friend, another night he would make a cutting remark that purposely hurt her.

By her second month of marriage, Rosalind was well and truly miserable, and she had not known what to do. She had made arrangements to go to the country while he was in London, but he wouldn't hear of it and forbade the servants from helping her make any arrangements to leave. So she had tried her best to stay out of his way, hurrying out of a room when he came in, keeping their time together to the short dinner hour.

At least he hadn't been physically abusive, but his words and actions hurt all the same. He had visited her bed a couple of times in their first weeks together but called her a "cold fish," apparently much preferring to frequent his brothels.

And then he was dead. Rosalind thought back to the funeral and Bart's words to her. Never again would she be trapped like that, she vowed. She had wept with frustration following it all, and she was still mortified, a year later, that William Elliot had found her. Out of everyone present, why did it have to be him? Rosalind had always thought him rather wonderful. In addition to his looks, he always had a light to his eyes and a good word to say about everyone. She should have married someone like him. But of course, he had never noticed her, preferring Olivia. Not that her friend realized it, but it was obvious to everyone else who was around the two of them.

Her musings were interrupted by the rocking of the carriage, her stomach lurching in response. They had hardly begun their journey and already she wanted to ask James to stop and let her out of this beast. But no, she would have to bear with it; otherwise they would be traveling for the entire day. Best to just get it over with.

So instead, she closed her eyes and willed herself to sleep.

4

Rosalind's eyes flew open as she was rocked forward in her seat, the carriage coming to a halt. She groaned as she felt her stomach heave, and she scrambled for the door handle, letting herself out just in time to be sick on the side of the road. She paused for a moment, doubled over as she gathered herself, taking deep breaths. As she opened her eyes, she nearly jumped at the pair of boots just inches away from her face.

She looked up slowly, taking in the male form in front of her. The man was dressed in buckskin breeches, with simply a waistcoat over his shirt. All thoughts on his attire fled, however, when her eyes came to his face and she gasped, for it was completely covered in fabric.

"Well, that is simply disgusting," came the voice from behind the material, causing Rosalind's rationality to override her panic for a moment. Why was a highwayman speaking in such cultured tones? She forgot the thought, however, as he reached out to tightly grip her arm and bring her to a standing position.

"Had I not just seen that display, I would think you

rather lovely," he said before forcing her back up against the carriage. Rosalind darted her head back and forth until she saw poor James, rope tied around his hands and feet where he was bound to a nearby tree.

"Who else is with you?"

"N-no one," she stammered out, her heart pounding so loudly she thought they must be able to hear it, as she realized now how stupid she had been to think she could travel for hours without incident. She was exactly what men like this were waiting for.

As the highwayman leaned into the carriage to assure himself she spoke the truth, Rosalind inched away from him as she began looking for means of escape. She saw a pair of horses by the side of the road, their reins looped around a tree branch. Perhaps — but no. A pair of horses meant that—

"Thinking of going somewhere, sweetheart?"

The second man, similarly dressed to the first, came from around the other side of the carriage, and Rosalind's heart sank. She could have possibly escaped one man, but two would be difficult. And she could never leave poor James behind.

She shook her head, and the two men stood and looked at her. Rosalind swallowed and tried not to show how frightened she was, clenching her fists at her side to keep them from shaking.

"I — I do not have anything you might want," she said. "All that is in my bag is a few dresses, a journal, and some books. I have nothing of value."

"Ah, come now, you in a fancy carriage like this, I'm sure there must be some pretty trinkets on your person, or some coins in a reticule stashed away, are there not?" The first man asked, coming to stand in front of her once more.

Rosalind ripped off her glove then worked her simple wedding band off her finger.

"Here, you can have this," she said, not caring at all if she never saw Harold's ring again. "That is the only jewelry I own."

Well, that was not quite true. She had her grandmother's necklace, in which a small ruby was inlaid, but it would have little value. Rosalind treasured it not for what price it could fetch but for the reminder of the woman she had loved very much.

The first man stepped toward her, taking the ring. He roughly took her fingers, stretching her hands out in front of her as he searched her for any other valuables. Rosalind noted, however, that he did take care to be as respectful as possible despite his actions, as if he had been raised to handle a lady with care. It slightly calmed her, and again, she wondered at the man's identity.

"Ah, what do we have here?" he asked, fingering the chain around her neck.

"N-nothing," she said. "Just an old family heirloom of no worth, I promise you. It will fetch hardly a pound were you to sell it, but it was my grandmother's you see, and I—"

Her words were choked off as he snapped the chain, inspecting the necklace before stuffing it into his pocket.

"Why would you take it?" Her words came out almost in a whisper, in disbelief at the man's cruelty.

"Why would you hide it, is the better question?" he asked her. "Watch her," he said to the second man before entering the carriage, where he must have been looking through the rest of her things before re-emerging, apparently frustrated in the fact that she was actually telling the truth regarding her lack of any valuables.

He walked down the path, kicking at stones and

muttering to himself as he seemed unable to decide what to do next. The man with Rosalind said nothing, but frowned after him, looking back and forth between the two of them.

"Can you not see that there is nothing left for you?" Rosalind asked him. "I think it would be best for you to let us be on our way, is it not? We will say nothing to anyone, I promise, and you can continue on. Let James and me go."

The man shook his head, and as the time stretched on, Rosalind found panic creeping in once more. If they weren't going to let her go, what else was there to do? They wouldn't ... get rid of her, would they? Oh God, she prayed silently. Please help us out of this.

The first man finally returned and strode toward them.

"We must leave," he said to his companion, and Rosalind felt her hopes soar, sending a prayer of thankfulness upward now. "But we will take the girl."

"What?" she gasped. "But why?"

"Clearly you are of a family of some means. If we request a ransom for you, someone is sure to pay it."

Rosalind let out a hoarse laugh. "Unfortunately, that is where you are sadly mistaken. You see, there is no one who cares enough to pay anything for me. My husband is dead, and my parents have no great feeling toward me. You would be better to leave me be."

"Your husband's estate, who owns it now?"

"His brother, and he could care less about me."

The man stared at her, his dark blue eyes glinting above the fabric that covered his face. There was something rather familiar about them, she thought, but she couldn't quite place where she might know them from.

"We shall see about that. Come."

Rosalind's heart beat fast as the other man pushed her toward the horses, pulling a knife out of his pocket and flashing it toward her, telling her that if she were to try to run, there would be consequences. If they sent word to Bart, she would be back to where she started — worse, even, for it would mean that she had no chance of escape, but would be beholden to him. She had to find her way out of this, she thought, as the man forced her onto the horse. But how?

WILLIAM STRODE down the hill next to his country manor, Friday at his heels, as the two of them searched for the groundskeeper. The estate grounds hadn't been well maintained while his father was in care of them, a fact his mother lamented. William himself liked them as they were, with the natural beauty of the grasses and the woodland beyond. With an upcoming house party, however, they could do with a bit of maintenance, and he would have to have a discussion with Creighton, the lazy oaf.

I should sack him, thought William of his groundskeeper, though he knew he would never have the heart to do so. The man had been with their family the whole of his life, and as inefficient as he was, to get rid of him now would be cruel.

Ah, well, he thought. It didn't matter much in the grand scheme of things, particularly when he had issues such as his brother to worry about it. He hadn't seen him in a couple of days now, and he hoped Alfred had not found himself embroiled in another scheme to cover up his first.

His attention was taken by a pounding of hooves coming up the drive, and he held a hand over his eyes to see who was coming. It was his brother's friend, Richard Abbotsford. William detested the man, although he realized he would likely feel the same about his brother if he wasn't his own kin.

"Southam!" the man said, panting as he slid off his horse. "You are required immediately."

"Is something the matter?" William asked, suddenly concerned that something had happened to Alfred. They had never been on the best of terms, true, but he was still his family. "Is my brother injured? Has there been an accident?"

"No, no, nothing like that," the man got out. "But he — that is, we have found ourselves in a spot of trouble."

William closed his eyes for a moment, as he dug deep to find patience with the two idiots who seemed to constantly be trying his patience.

"And what, pray tell, type of trouble would this be?"

The man shifted his weight back and forth between his feet, unwilling to meet William's gaze. "I think it would be best that Alfred tells you himself. Or ... perhaps shows you."

Resigned, William turned back toward the house, making his way back up the hill to saddle his horse. With Friday running beside him, he followed Richard down the road, away from the estate. He was surprised when the man took him through his own lands, deeper into the woods. They were in hunting territory now, where William had planned to lead his house party this weekend. He was quite looking forward to having guests, although for the moment he cleared his mind from anything but whatever it was his brother had gotten himself into.

They came upon a clearing leading to one of the hunting cabins in the woods. It had been the home of the gamekeeper at one point but had been long neglected as the man currently holding the position lived in the nearby town with his family.

"What is going on, Richard?" William asked through tight lips, his impatience growing by the moment. Richard's face had gone rather pale, and his gaze was now affixed to the cottage, where Alfred stepped out of the door.

"William," he said with a nod, although he did not seem pleased to see him, despite the fact he had asked him to come out here. "I've got myself in a situation."

"So it seems," William said, dismounting and crossing his arms over his chest in impatience. "Would you suppose to tell me what that particular situation is?"

"Well you see, I, ah, when you would not loan me the money I needed, I became rather desperate."

"Go on."

"So, for the past week or so, Richard and I .... well, that is..."

"You will have to tell me sooner or later, Alfred, so it might as well be now, before you waste any more of my time."

"We've been robbing coaches."

"What?" William asked, looking at his brother in shock. As the words registered, he exploded, rocking forward toward his brother, pushing him back against the wood of the cottage. "What's wrong with you, man? You are the son of a viscount! My God, Alfred...."

He released his brother, raising a hand to his head as it began to throb with the familiar ache brought on by Alfred. William began to pace in the dirt as his brother continued talking.

"What else was I to do?" Alfred asked, holding his hands out in front of him. "I asked you for help, and you refused."

"For good reason!" William cried. "Do not make this my fault, Alfred. This is of your own stupidity. Now, what happened? Did someone find you out?"

"Not exactly...."

"Then what?"

"Well, we came upon a carriage, a very well-to-do carriage, mind you, and inside was a woman — alone. We tied up her driver, searched her and her belongings, and found almost nothing."

"Please tell me you released her unharmed."

Alfred tensed. "Well, a woman like that, we thought surely someone would be willing to pay to have her returned, so we ... we took her."

William prayed he had heard the words wrong. He stopped walking back and forth and turned to his brother, his gaze intent upon him. "What do you mean you took her?"

"I mean, we took her at knifepoint, brought her ... here ... to the cottage, and then we looked for her relatives. Unfortunately, it was as she said. Her husband is dead, and his brother now has the title, but upon asking around, it seems the estate has been left with nothing. She did not even receive a stipend from which to live off."

"Allow me to guess the next part of this plot, Alfred. The woman is now in the hunting cottage, has seen your face, and you do not know what to do with her. You do not — thank God — have the stomach to kill her, and yet you also do not want to release her. And so you summoned me."

"That's about the way of it, yes," Alfred said, looking relieved as though he thought this meant that William was now going to take care of it.

"I have news for you, Alfred," William said. "This is not my problem, and I am not going to do anything about it."

"What do you mean?" Alfred looked shocked. "What am I supposed to do?"

"I don't know! Not rob coaches? Not make irresponsible

bets or investments? Find yourself a regular living? Live as a man of your station should? Whatever you do, I told you before, Alfred, and I will tell you again, it is none of my concern anymore."

William turned to walk away when he heard banging on the door.

"Help!" came a female voice from inside. "Please, whoever is out there, let me go!"

He stopped with a sigh and turned back around to face his brother.

"How long has she been here?"

"How long?"

"Yes, you fool, how long?"

"A couple of days."

"A couple of *days*? Have you been feeding her?"

"Of course!" Alfred had the audacity to look indignant. "What do you take me for?"

William could not bring himself to answer the question, but, sighing in resolution at his own softheartedness, he strode toward the hunting cottage and pulled open the door.

And found himself staring, in shock, into a pair of very familiar green eyes inside a small, pretty face.

5

"Mr. Elliot? That is, I mean, Lord Southam? I—"

"I hardly think we need to concern ourselves with social politeness at the moment," he responded wryly, as Rosalind found herself staring at him in utter shock, closing her mouth when she realized it was hanging open. "Good Lord. Rosalind."

"William, I — oh, I am so happy to see you!" She didn't think about what she was doing, but flung herself in her arms, relieved that somehow he — inexplicably — had come to her rescue. She reveled in his warmth, feeling his hard chest against her, but quickly stepped back, realizing that no matter the circumstances, she had gone far beyond the bounds of propriety. "I am so sorry. It is simply that I am so grateful you are here. I have no idea *why* you are here, but somehow you are. You see, my coach was attacked by highwaymen, and I was taken here, to this shack. They mean to ransom for me, but they do not seem to be aware that no one will care. Thank—"

"Please," he cut her off, and she realized she was blathering like an idiot. "Stop thanking me."

"Why ever not? The fact that you found me—"

"I did not find you," he said with a shake of his head.

"Whatever do you mean?" she asked, confused by his response. "Well, where am I then?"

"You are on my land."

"Your land? But ... but how...?" She watched him as he joined her in the cottage, striding back and forth in front of her as he rubbed at his temples.

"Your abductor ... was my brother. Alfred!" he called out the open door. "Perhaps we should all come inside."

"No!" she said, shaking her head fiercely as she pushed her way out the cottage door, nearly tripping as the sun hit her full in the face, almost blinding her after the near darkness of the room. "I am *not* returning to that shack."

She shook the fog from her head as she tried to understand the situation. Alfred Elliot, the brother of William, a man she had known nearly her entire life, had robbed her carriage and abducted her, holding her ransom on William's land? She had met Alfred before but had never known him well. What was the meaning of all of this? It was utterly unheard of.

"You didn't ... that is, did you know, of what, of me, I..." The words came out of her mouth garbled, and Rosalind closed her eyes, willing it all away. This was ultimately her own fault. She should have had more sense when she made her travel plans. She should not have been as proud as she was, and should have taken a mail coach. Or asked Olivia's husband to come accompany her. But now....

"No, of course, I knew nothing of this," William said as if sensing her distress. "Lady Templeton, I cannot begin to tell you how sorry I am for all that has happened to you. I know that there is no way to properly make amends, but if you come to the house, we can discuss this civilly, I promise you that."

She eyed Alfred, who was standing to the side, arms crossed over his chest as he looked everywhere but at her.

"Alfred will not hurt you again," he added, and she turned to look pointedly at Alfred's accomplice.

"Nor will Richard," added William, and she caught his glare toward the man.

"Very well, Lord Southam," she finally responded. She didn't want to agree, she didn't want to go anywhere with any of these men, but at the moment she saw no other choice.

He led her over to his horse, and she was reminded of two days ago, when Alfred made her ride with him. It made sense now why Alfred had looked so familiar. He had the same deep blue eyes as William, his sandy hair a slightly darker shade of red and a little less controlled than William's, but that unique color all the same. She had met Alfred before, she recalled, but only very briefly.

She stepped toward the horse, finally completing the internal war that raged within her. For at the end of it all, where else was she to go?

If anything, this proved what she had come to realize with Harold. No one could ever truly be trusted, for more often than not, people hid their true selves from all around them — even family and fiancées.

She put her hands on the horse's flank and was about to mount when she suddenly heard a great thrashing in the greenery to her left.

"What is that—"

She had no time to react as the giant dog came bounding of the brush. It swiveled its head from side to side as if assessing the situation before running up to Rosalind and leaping up on her, his great paws coming to her shoulders. Rosalind staggered back, nearly falling but managing to catch herself before she tumbled.

William shouted to the dog as he raced toward them, but stopped suddenly when Rosalind waved him back.

She reached out and scratched the giant beast between the ears, and it seemed to calm him as he leaned into her, apparently enjoying her touch as he gave her a big lick on the cheek. She laughed then, some of the tension of the situation abating, and she looked up to find William staring at her in astonishment.

"What is it?" she asked.

William looked down at her. "He typically doesn't like anyone ... except me. Apparently, now you as well."

She didn't know what to say to that, so she turned her attention back to the dog, taking strength from him as she brought her nose to his. She finally straightened and turned to William.

"Very well, then. Let's go."

He nodded, and she walked to him stiffly, hoping that he realized just how angry she still was.

When he placed his hands around her waist to help her up onto the horse, however, her reaction to him was nothing like it had been toward Alfred when he had done the same — far from it, in fact. Where Alfred's touch had been sent shivers of disgust up her spine, William's hands on her *did* make her tingle ... but in a decidedly different way.

Once she was on, he mounted behind her, his body encompassing hers, his arm around her waist, and she wanted to lean back into the closeness of his hard chest.

She told her body — and possibly her heart — to stop

being such a traitor, and resolved to feel nothing but anger toward these men. She said not a word over the short ride to the house, holding herself stiff and straight, as far from the man as possible.

~

William could not convince her to believe him that he could make amends.

"My brother was desperate," he said, pacing around the bright study, the drapes pulled back to let the light in upon an oak table, tan leather wingback chairs, and the walls, papered in a mint green. "And desperate men do things they would never normally do."

"That matters not," she said quietly from her seat across the desk. Her small frame seemed dwarfed by the chair, and he winced at the dark circles under her eyes. "No matter what the circumstance, there is always an honorable away. Desperation is no excuse."

"You are right," he said with a sight frown, sighing as he came to a stop and threw himself into the chair matching hers. "There is nothing I can do to change the past, and I am sorry my brother did this to you. All I can promise is to do what I can to make it right."

"And you would do that by...?"

"I am not sure," he said, rubbing at his temples once again. Once the ache set in, it was hard to be rid of it for the remainder of the day. "Is there anything you need? Anything I can do for you?"

She was silent for a moment, her eyes narrowing as she retreated into her own thoughts.

"Can you make sure that James is all right following the incident?" she finally asked, to which he was confused.

"Who is James?"

"The driver of my carriage. Last I saw him, he was tied in rope underneath a tree."

"Oh dear God," William said, still hardly believing that the acts they were discussing were perpetrated by his brother. "Absolutely. I will speak to Alfred as to what he did with the man. I sincerely hope he simply released him and he returned to your home. Why, even now, likely someone is looking for you."

Her head snapped up at that, and he didn't miss the look of fear that crossed her face before she quickly turned her face away.

"I must ask, Lady Rosalind ... why were you traveling unaccompanied, and to where were you going?"

When she said nothing, his gaze followed hers to her hands, which were twisting the material of her dress round and round her fingers. Clearly he had agitated the woman even further, though how he wasn't sure.

He hastily added, "I do not mean to pry. I am simply ascertaining how I can help you reach whatever destination to which you were attempting to travel."

She retained her look of concern, but cleared her throat and met his stare, which he hoped was encouraging, before breaking her eyes away, allowing them to flit about the room.

"I was going to visit Olivia — that is, the Duke and Duchess of Breckenridge."

He nodded. "Were they aware of your impending arrival?"

"No," she said with a quick shake of her head. "It was ... to be a surprise of sorts."

Clearly, something more was at play here, something of which she did not care to speak. She obviously didn't trust him, though William didn't blame her after all that Alfred had done to her. He wanted to help her, but first he would have to convince her to let him.

"I will have word sent round to Oliv— the Duke and Duchess that they can expect you soon. You are most welcome to stay here, and then I will personally accompany you once we receive word that they are in residence."

"In residence — oh, I had never considered that they wouldn't be," she said, her eyes widening, "How very stupid of me. Of course I should have written Olivia first. It is just, you see, that I left somewhat hastily, and so, as I know that Olivia was not in London, I simply assumed she was in the countryside..."

"It's no matter," he said, trying to reassure her. She was a slight thing, but she looked even more drawn than he had remembered her. Perhaps the tragedy of losing her husband had taken its toll on her over the past year.

They were both quiet for a moment, clearly contemplating the severity of all that had happened.

"Well then," he said, filling the silence. "Why do we not see to finding you a bedchamber, for tonight at least. I'll have my housekeeper prepare a room."

"There is one thing," she said, setting her chin resolutely. "I will not stay under the same roof as your brother. I know this is his home, but I cannot — I should not be able to sleep. If he must stay, then I will look for other lodging for tonight."

"That is understandable," he responded, sighing inwardly. It only made sense for her to ask it of him, but it was somewhat inconvenient, as they were in the middle of the countryside. "I'll speak with him. Why don't you wait here for a moment? I'll have a tray sent in for you, and then Mrs. Cranbourn will make sure you are comfortable."

"Thank you," she said, quietly.

The pounding in his head increasing with every breath now, he tried not to let the pain on his face show as he walked out of the room.

6

Rosalind felt all of the tension that she had been holding in release as he left, and she sank back into the chair. She hated conflict, and had always done her best to avoid any sort of confrontation, be it with her parents, her husband, or anyone else who had crossed her path.

She should be livid with all of the Elliots for what Alfred had done to her, and yet, she had been as agreeable as ever with William. Not only that, but she had thanked him — thanked him! The words had come, unbidden, from her mouth before she had even time to consider what she was saying.

She collapsed her head forward into her hands with a groan.

She was awkward enough in a regular social situation. Oh, she knew how to make polite conversation, was aware of what she was supposed to say and when she should refrain from speaking. It was in these more intimate conversations with people, particularly people she did not know very well, that she often struggled to find the right words, the words that she felt would truly portray what she was feeling.

After an exchange had concluded, she always knew what she *ought* to have said. Even now, she longed to be able to revisit her conversation with William and tell him just how frightened she had been when his brother had held her captive in the hunting cottage, how desperate she had been for escape, and how worried she had been that Bart actually would come to collect her. But no, she had simply sat there like an idiot, nodding and agreeing with nearly every word he said.

Perhaps it was because William was every bit as handsome and agreeable as he had always been. True, he wasn't classically good-looking, but his features suited him. His light brown hair was tinted red and was given to a slight curl, his eyes so deep a blue they made many a woman envious. His smile came quickly and frequently, and he loved to laugh and generally enjoy life.

It was likely why he had always been so drawn to Olivia. As a girl, Rosalind had watched him closely, longing for his affections, and instead had simply been more attuned to the way his gaze followed Olivia everywhere she went. Not that she blamed him. Olivia was not only striking, but she had a way about her that drew people. She said what she wanted, when she felt it, and cared not what others thought of her.

Was it age, her friend's marriage, or perhaps the responsibilities of the estate, however, that had brought more lines to William's face than she remembered, more tension to his bearing that he had never previously held?

Her ears perked at voices in the hallway. They were murmurs at first, but as their speakers drew closer to the door, she closed her eyes and made not a sound as she tried to concentrate on what they were saying.

"Alfred, for the duration of time Lady Templeton is here, you shall have to leave," came William's voice, as even and tempered as it always was.

"Leave?" Alfred's bellow sounded incredulous. "But where should I go?"

"I am not sure .... perhaps the hunting cottage?"

"The hunting shack?"

"Yes, the hunting shack," William repeated. "You seemed to think it was appropriate quarters for Lady Templeton, so I am sure it will do just fine for you as well."

"William, be reasonable," a cutting, female voice chimed in. This must be his mother, thought Rosalind. She had met Lady Southam a handful of times, none of the experiences being particularly agreeable. "You simply cannot send your brother away."

"Mother, please tell me you are not condoning Alfred's actions. What he did was unspeakable. Why—"

"You put him in rather a precarious position, did you not?"

Rosalind's eyes widened at the woman's words. What was wrong with this family?

"Enough!" William sounded angrier than she had ever heard him, and the other voices ceased. "Alfred, for the time being, you cannot stay in this house. Find somewhere else. Mother, I will hear none of your protestations. They will not sway me."

At that, she heard a bellow of anger, and then loud footsteps retreating down the hallway.

Moments later, William re-entered the room, his face drawn. Rosalind noticed that he continued to rub at his forehead and his temples, and she wondered if he were suffering a megrim.

"Are you all right?" she asked, and he looked up in astonishment, as if he had forgotten she was there.

"Yes, yes, fine," he said, his words now short and terse, which made her pause. Normally he was one of the most affable, kind men she had ever met. Although clearly the situation was one that would test the limits of anyone, no matter how normally considerate one was.

He walked to the windows, pulling the curtains closed, before rounding his desk once more and sitting down heavily.

"Alfred will be gone from the house within the hour, so you need not worry," he said briskly, as if trying to work his way through the situation as quickly as possible. "I will write a note to the Duke and Duchess of Breckenridge as we speak, and the housekeeper, Mrs. Cranbourn, will be in to collect you shortly. Ah, here is a tea tray for you in the meantime."

He beckoned the maid in with the tray and took a piece of paper from a desk drawer before dipping his quill pen in the ink blotter and beginning to scratch out his note.

More for something with which to keep herself busy rather than having a need for it, Rosalind poured herself a cup of tea. She didn't mind tea, but she actually much preferred coffee. She typically didn't ask for it, however, not wanting anyone to have to go to the trouble of preparing it just for her. She realized as she looked at the tray that she *was* rather hungry, and she appreciated the pastries in front of her.

"Would you like a cup of tea, my lord?" she asked, to which he simply shook his head, and she began to be rather affronted by his manner. It wasn't as if *she* had done anything wrong in this situation.

Finished with his note, he sat back and found an envelope, sealing it with his stamp.

Rosalind looked at him over her tea cup. There was something she needed to know, as much as she did not particularly want to ask.

"Did ... did Alfred mention what exactly was said when he contacted my family regarding my ransom?" she asked, dismayed when his deep blue eyes met hers and she saw the pity within them.

"He did," he responded slowly, as if trying to determine what to say to her.

"They cared naught, did they?" she asked, more as a statement than a question.

"It seems your parents determined that you were now the responsibility of the current Earl of Templeton," he said with a sign. "And Bartholomew Branson, now Lord Templeton and brother of your late husband, of course, demanded your return but said he had no funds with which to pay anything for you."

"I see," she said, her cheeks warming in embarrassment. "That would be as I would have expected. No matter. Would you mind ensuring that Bart does not learn of my current whereabouts?"

William cocked his head as he looked at her, as if wanting to know more.

"Are you in some sort of trouble, Lady Templeton?"

He was being kind, she knew, and would help her if she asked for it, but the man had barely looked at her their entire lives. Now that it was just the two of them, together in this study, she was not going to further his pity for her and her current situation. Besides, what could he do, besides help her make her way to Olivia's?

As she contemplated what to say to him, she saw his

eyes flick to the open door, where a woman, likely the housekeeper, awaited her.

Rosalind rose, feeling herself dismissed, but not before William's low voice reached her.

"If you need anything, Lady Templeton, please just ask."

"It's Rosalind," she said with a nod, then followed the housekeeper out the door.

The Southam manor might not have been as impressive as some of the other country homes she had visited, but Rosalind found that there was something rather ... cheerful about it. It was filled with color, both on the walls and within the Aubusson carpets lining the floors. Each room seemed to be decorated in a different hue, but whether it was red or blue or green, large windows emitted plenty of light, and white wainscoting softened the intensity. Paintings were primarily floral patterns or natural landscapes. Even William's ancestors looked down at her with what appeared to be smiles on their faces.

Apparently, whoever had decorated the house also had a voice in the landscaping of the grounds, for Rosalind could see the natural views through the many windows as she walked along.

The room she had been given was primarily white, accented in blue — a pretty wallpaper with an azure floral pattern on white lined walls, while the bed linens were, on closer inspection, a blue so pale they looked almost a neutral color. The furniture was beautiful — this room had obviously been designed for a lady, with a mahogany fauteuil open-armed wood chair placed in front of a toilet.

She sank down onto the upholstered seat and looked into the plate glass surrounded by brass ornamentation.

She looked pale, she noted, and pinched her cheeks to try to bring some color into them. She had been staring into the beautiful eyes of William Elliot, and now that she looked at her own, she grimaced. They were a green, yes, but a rather dull green. They could possibly be called gray, she thought, and seemed to even have a bit of blue in them on occasion, but not a very nice blue. Overall, they were nothing of note, and she wrinkled her nose up at them and turned away. Her entire face, actually, was rather plain. It was not that she wasn't pretty, she thought, it's just that she wasn't really memorable either. She just ... was.

Oh, she supposed she shouldn't be so hard on herself, she thought, rising out of the chair and walking to the window. She had just been so used to her mother pointing out her flaws throughout her entire life that now she always noted them herself.

Mrs. Cranbourn had left her valise in the corner of the room but had not unpacked anything. That was a job for her lady's maid, but she, of course, did not currently have one. Thank goodness that Alfred and his friend had taken the bag from the carriage in hopes to find something valuable within it. It was not so much the clothing Rosalind needed, although it was helpful to not have to find new attire. No, it was what else the small bag held.

She reached her hand through the layers of fabric until her fingers hit the dark, hard shell of a book. Rosalind drew it out, finding it was not what she was looking for. It took another three volumes until she smiled, seeing the journal in front of her. All was not lost after all, she thought.

7

Dinner with William Elliot, Viscount of Southam, was an event that Rosalind had dreamt about in the past, if she were being honest.

In her dreams, however, she and William were smiling at one another over the candlelit dining table, content in the company of one another and the love they shared.

This dinner was altogether different. They sat across from one another, but the air was tense and she was unsure of what to speak about. *So, my lord, please tell me more about your brother who abducted me?* Hardly. Or, *what did you think of Olivia's wedding last year? Did it upset you?* She thought not. Or she could ask him, *How well did you know my husband? Did you frequent the same brothels? Do you know his brother, who is trying to marry me and make the rest of my life entirely miserable, more so than it would have been even with Harold?* Not exactly polite dinner conversation.

And then there was his mother.

Lady Southam sat beside William, the cold pale blue of her eyes, so unlike William's warm ones, piercing into Rosalind. The woman said nothing, but rather simply stared at her, as if trying to disconcert her. Rosalind did not want to admit how well it was working.

Rosalind cleared her throat. "'Tis lovely weather we are having, is it not?"

William looked at her through hooded eyes. "It is, Lady Templeton. The spring has been rather warm this year, and I think the summer should be equally as pleasant."

She nodded, wishing that this was over, that she could soon be on her way to see Olivia. If her friend was here, she would know how to fill this conversation with words that actually mattered. Despite the atmosphere of the room, the setting was rather lovely. The walls of the dining room were a pale yellow, with paintings of daisies and fields of sunflowers upon the walls. She looked forward to seeing it in the brightness of the daylight sun.

At the moment, the viscount did not seem particularly thrilled to be having dinner with her, as he was silent and hardly ate. She noted he simply moved the food around on his plate.

"I must tell you that I do have some news," he said, and she looked up at him.

"As you know," he continued, "The home of the Duke and Duchess of Breckenridge is but a couple of hours away. The messenger I sent earlier this morning has already returned. It seems that they have departed for a time to Bath, and are not thought to return for a few weeks."

Her fork clattered to the plate. Olivia hadn't mentioned to her that she was going anywhere — but then, why would she? Rosalind had given her no reason to believe that she would be seeing her at any time in the near future. In fact, she had hardly spent time with any of her acquaintances. Most of them were now married, and she did not want to foist her problems upon them. Spending time with the happy couples was also rather difficult, though Rosalind knew she must set her own envious feelings aside and simply be happy for them.

No matter — at the moment, she had to determine what she had best do now.

"I should be happy to provide you transportation to wherever else it is you wish to go," William continued. "Back to London? To your country home? Perhaps—"

"No," she said, with more force that she had meant and her next words came rather softly. "That is, no thank you. It's just that I ... I have nowhere else to go."

"Whatever do you mean?" he asked, gazing intently at her as his mother snorted and raised her eyebrows incredulously.

"At the moment I ... I simply have no other option," she said, not wanting to explain to him — or, more particularly his mother — her circumstances. William said nothing for a moment, but simply stared at her as if he was trying to will her to open up, but she was resolute. She did not want him to be concerned with her problems. They were for her to deal with.

"Well, then, I do have a solution for you — at the moment," he said, seemingly frustrated, although she was grateful he didn't press the matter. "I am to be having a house party this week. You are welcome to stay throughout the gathering. Although you are a widow and my mother is in residence, it would be rather untoward otherwise for the two of us to be staying here together. However, it will be no matter if there are other guests in the house."

"William," his mother finally spoke, interrupting him. "I should hardly think that Lady Templeton would want to be part of a house party at this time. Why, she is barely out of mourning and—"

"Thank you for your offer," Rosalind said quietly, and the woman raised her eyebrows at her. "I will stay."

She really had no other option.

"Well," his mother said with a harumph. "It seems no one cares any longer what I think. There is something you must understand, Lady Templeton. You cannot banish my son. The guests will be expecting Alfred, and he would dearly love to return to the party."

Rosalind felt her heart beat faster at the woman's words, and she looked at William imploringly. He sighed.

"Alfred committed a terrible crime, it is true, although what my mother says must be considered," he said. "I have determined, however, that if you would like me to ask him to leave my home, I am more than willing to do so. What he did to you is unforgivable. It is likely, however, that he will make accusations against you, and your name may be brought into similar disrepute. I would do all I could to prevent that from happening, but it is a risk. And so I ask you, Lady Templeton, what would you like me to do?"

She wanted to tell him to send Alfred away, to make him pay for what he did. Yet she realized that if he did so, in all likelihood Bart would find out where Alfred had taken her, where she was currently residing. And so, she made the cowardly decision, one to protect herself.

"He can stay," she choked out, and William nodded, his face serious while a gloating smile spread across his mother's wide face.

"He will, then, be once again residing in the manor house," he said. "You understand that?"

"I do," she nodded, and began pushing around her own food, no longer hungry.

The sooner she could be finished this awkward dinner, the better.

William cursed as he stumbled to his room. He had only just managed to make it through that blasted dinner. He felt like a lout, knowing he had been short with Rosalind and had allowed his mother to be condescending toward her. Rosalind deserved much better treatment from his family, particularly after all she had been put through at the hands of his brother.

He had told Alfred in no uncertain terms that his thievery was to stop *now*. All that he had stolen was to be on William's desk in the morning. William would do all he could to return the possessions to their owners. Alfred told him much of it had been sold, but he agreed he would do what he could to help return the remainder. William saw the glint in his eye and knew that likely he would only receive that which had turned out to hold little value, but he was unsure of what else he could do. He had no desire to bail his brother out yet again, but he must right his actions.

William had hardly been able to speak tonight due to the pounding in his head. All he had wanted through that entire dinner was to return to his room, to close his eyes, and slink into the dark of night.

The headaches had begun years ago, although it seemed the older he became, the more intense they were, brought on more frequently by stressful situations — such as the one he currently found himself in. He threw a hand over his eyes as he fell back on his bed.

If only he could keep them at bay until the end of this party, he thought as he reached for the glass of brandy on his nightstand. Keep it together, William, he told himself. He heard a soft scratch on the door, and his valet entered. Roberts had been with him for years and knew what ailed his master. Without words he helped him undress and get into bed. He took the only lit candle in the room with him, shutting the door quietly behind him and allowing William to fall into a deep, dreamless sleep.

THE NEXT DAY DAWNED BRIGHT, and William felt great relief upon waking to discover that the pounding pain had left his head, and he felt much more refreshed. Thank God, he thought in genuine gratefulness. The longest a headache had ever lasted had been three days, and it had nearly broken him.

His good mood remained until he entered the breakfast room and found his brother and his mother sitting at the table across from Rosalind. The three sat there, Alfred with a smirk on his face, his mother with a self-satisfied smile, and a silent Rosalind wearing a mask of tight composure. He sighed. Somehow he didn't think this was going to go well.

"Good morning Mother, Lady Templeton," he said, making his way over to the sideboard and heaping a plate with eggs, ham, and toast. "Alfred." He found that after his headache subsided he often had quite an appetite, likely because he usually wasn't able to eat much while in the throes of it.

"Good morning, William," Alfred said heartily. "How do you fare this fine day?"

"I am well," he said. "What are you doing here, Alfred? I thought you were staying ... elsewhere until the party."

"I was," he said, "But Mother invited me in for breakfast. Is there anything wrong with that? As you have enough food here to feed an entire party, I believe I can partake, can I not? Besides that, our guests will be arriving in but a few days, which is soon enough."

William inclined his head in recognition of his words as he set down his plate, and pulled out his chair.

"Are you well this morning, Lady Templeton?" he asked, taking a closer look at Rosalind. Her face was pale and drawn, and he realized that while he understood her reluctance of wanting to be in the presence of Alfred, with his own ailment yesterday he hadn't really thought much about her entire ordeal and how much it would have frightened her. These were treacherous waters, and he wasn't entirely sure how to navigate them. There was that feeling again pulling at him, but stronger this time, that made him want to reach out, wrap his arms around her and protect her from any and all that threatened to do her harm. And she was, he realized, rather lovely. His sentiments rather shocked him, and he didn't know what to make of them. He shook them off and focused on her words.

"Good morning Lord Southam," she said tightly but kept her eyes down on her plate, which looked untouched. It seemed that when the woman did not feel comfortable, she withdrew into herself, and William wasn't quite sure how to draw her out.

"Speaking of the upcoming party," Alfred said, "Will the future Viscountess of Southam be one of our guests?"

That seemed to catch Rosalind's attention, as her head snapped up to look back and forth between Alfred and William.

"Are you looking for a wife, my lord?" she asked, her eyes wide.

William cleared his throat. This wasn't a conversation he felt like having in front of Rosalind, although he wasn't quite certain why that would be so.

"I am not entirely sure," he said after a moment of hesitation. "I suppose it is time I found a wife, although I do not exactly want to force the issue."

"William has had a difficult time finding anyone to measure up to his goddess, Lady Olivia," said Alfred, a smirk crossing his face, which William wanted to reach over and smack.

Instead he tried to maintain calm. "Alfred, you are now fabricating something that is simply not true."

"No? You mean you can tell me with all honesty that you have not spent your life in love with a woman who sees you as nothing more than a friend?" Alfred let out a laugh that sent sparks of irritation up and down William's spine. He wanted to shake his brother, but doing so would only prove him right.

"I am sure Lady Templeton is not particularly enjoying listening to the bantering between us."

"No? She looks rather interested, are you not, Lady Templeton?" They both looked over at Rosalind, who had her hands folded in her lap, seemingly disinterested, although William could see her studying him out of the corner of her eye.

"I am sure that whatever your interests or intentions may be, they are certainly none of my concern," she said, with the politeness he knew she had been raised to portray. As much as he realized this was the way of women in society, he longed for her to shed the facade and tell him with blunt openness exactly what she thought.

"Well, let me tell you, Lady Templeton, our William here has always fancied himself in love with your good friend. Alas, now that she is married, he will have to look elsewhere, no?" Alfred continued on, as William's grip tightened on his fork. He felt the dull throb beginning in the back of his head, and he closed his eyes, trying to will it away. "Anyway, fortunately for him, Lady Diana Watson will be attending our little party and, while perhaps not *quite* as striking and forthright as Lady Olivia, she is, at the very least, of a similar pattern as her, is she not, William?"

"She is," added his mother with a smile when he said nothing. "You will quite enjoy her company William, I am sure."

"I hardly know the woman, Mother, Alfred," he said, glaring at the two of them in turn from across the round table. "And, as I mentioned, this is not a conversation that Lady Templeton is interested in listening to for many reasons, but certainly first and foremost that none of it is true nor has any bearing on the future. I have no feelings for the Duchess of Breckenridge besides that of a longstanding friend, and I shall marry when I feel the opportunity presents itself. Now, perhaps we should move on to another subject, all right? Such as the fact that, Alfred, I wish you had not returned to the house until I had asked it of you."

Alfred sighed and shook his head in mockery of him. "Come, now, brother, what are you going to do with me? You know to tell anyone of the happenings would only put a stain on the reputation of our dear Lady Templeton here, and you wouldn't want that, would you, my lady? Now, if you want to change subjects, my dear brother, I am interested in learning more about this woman in our midst. Tell me, Lady Templeton, are you enjoying your stay?"

William saw a pink stain begin to seep into Rosalind's cheeks as she looked up at Alfred, her eyes casting daggers that she did not put into words. "Your brother has been more than kind," she said tersely. "And I appreciate his invitation to stay for the upcoming party."

"Well, it's not as if you have much choice, do you?"

Alfred asked, leering at her. "For as you well know, no one else cares enough to take you."

William was about to admonish his brother when an icy gleam filled Rosalind's eyes, and she leaned toward him over the table. "I am making my own way in the world, Mr. Elliot, instead of leeching off my family members or committing crimes in order to sustain myself."

Well, well. So the woman did have some backbone. Brava, Rosalind, William thought. Unfortunately, her words seemed to fuel the flame of Alfred's disdain.

"I must tell you, Lady Templeton, I had the *privilege* of knowing your late husband. We frequented the same ... establishments, if you will. I hear tell he had a penchant for certain forms of entertainment that I should not like to speak about in polite company. I suppose that is why he spent so much time away from the bedroom at home, for he was likely unable to find himself satisfied by his dear lady wife, eh?"

"That is enough," said William, pointing a finger in anger at his brother. "I have put up with your barbs long enough this morning. There will be no more of this, Alfred, or I will truly take all away from you — this home and access to any funds or support whatsoever. Do you hear me?"

Alfred glared at him with eyes so similar to his own, but he finally broke the stare, apparently admitting defeat — for the moment.

"Fine, William, if you are going to be that way," he said. "Though I only speak the truth. Is that not what you have always said you prefer? The truth from one's lips rather than what one feels you may want to hear? Well, anyway, it was lovely speaking with you, Lady Templeton. I hope you have a wonderful morning. Mother, good day."

With that, he rose and exited the room, humming a tune as he continued down the corridor.

"I believe I shall excuse myself as well," said Lady Southam, rising, seeming to have thoroughly enjoyed her breakfast and the conversation, as she left the room with a self-satisfied air.

William took a breath, feeling the tension that remained in the room following their departures. He finally looked at Rosalind, who sat unmoving, her hands clutched tightly in her lap, her gaze looking out over the table to the window at the peaceful lands stretching out below them in sharp contrast to the rockiness that Alfred had left in the room.

"I do apologize, Lady Templeton," William finally said. "Alfred has always lacked manners, of course, but this was beyond reproach. Forgive me for placing you in such a situation?"

She finally turned to look at him, and he was taken aback for a moment by the storm that was rolling through her sea green eyes. He had never really noticed them, before, he realized, but now the turbulence within them reached out and captured his attention, causing him to feel that rather strange and unexpected longing to do what he could to ease the pain.

"I believe I am no longer particularly hungry," she said. "Though I do have an urge to explore your lands. If you will excuse me?"

He could do nothing but nod, and when she left he sighed, his shoulders slumping. He had certainly entered into a rather trying situation. The question was, how was he to get himself out of it?

8

The moment Rosalind exited the dining room and was out of William's sight, she fled down the hallway, practically breaking into a run at her desire to be free from the room, with the echoes of Alfred's taunts in her ears, and the reminders that she would never be the type of woman a man like William Elliot would want.

In fact, she wasn't a woman who she felt any man was particularly drawn to. She knew she was pretty enough, but she wasn't a woman that men were attracted to at first sight. Her face never drew attention, nor hardly ever a second look. How often had she been introduced to the same people over and over again who had completely forgotten ever meeting her, as she had clearly been so unassuming and uninteresting?

William had remembered her well enough as Olivia's friend, but other than that she knew he had hardly any recollection of her, and rather had extended his invitation to her out of politeness as well as guilt over what his brother had done to her.

She made it to her room, shutting the door behind her

and leaning against it for a moment to collect herself. After a time, her breathing slowed and she felt a need for air. She found her journal in her pile of books, and taking it in hand, she meandered through the house until she found the library. She gathered a quill pen and ink pot from a desk in the corner and made her way to the beautiful terrace doors which opened to the grounds beyond.

Just a few steps, and as Rosalind walked into the sunshine, the warmth of it invaded her soul, and she finally, for a moment, felt peace settle over her. She basked in it for just a moment, forgetting all of the worry and all of the pain that had overcome her.

The muslin of her lavender skirts swept through the long grasses of the yard that was not particularly well maintained but held a certain bold wildness that was utterly refreshing.

If only the house was free of Alfred and Lady Southam, how perfectly peaceful it would be. Perhaps in her time here, Rosalind could complete the manuscript she was working on, then find a way to sell it and begin to support herself.

It was ironic, she thought, that despite the fact she could hardly think of what to say to others in the moment, when she wrote, thoughts came tumbling out onto the page, and she was able to give her characters the words that she so longed to be able to use herself. She had been writing for some time now, though primarily for enjoyment. Now, she was determined that she would support herself with her work. It was simply a matter of finding the right connections to help her with it. For that, she would have to make her way to London and find a place to stay. Once Olivia returned, she would ask for her assistance and for use of her London residence. Until then, she would make do with her current situation.

She found a beautiful oak by a small pond and leaned against its trunk, it's large branches shading her with leaves that rustled in the slight wind. Rosalind took a deep breath, drinking in the peace the outdoors brought her, and opened her notebook. She dipped her pen in the ink and brought it to the page, where the words began to seemingly write themselves as she poured out her heartbreak and pain, allowing her a sense of release.

She didn't know how long she sat there, thinking and writing, her emotions working their way into a story that flowed without much effort on her part. Sometimes, it seemed, the words wrote themselves, the characters acting upon their own will. She loved those days, though she could never predict when they would come; rather she had to work within them when the opportunity presented itself.

She was so intent on her work that she let out a shriek of surprise when she suddenly felt a warm, hairy body leaning against her, a warm tongue upon her cheek.

"Oh, it's you!" she said with a bit of a laugh of relief when she turned to find the dog next to her. "I am so sorry, I didn't notice you."

She reached out, rubbing the dog's head, her fingers scratching him where he seemed to enjoy it between his ears. "You are a lovely one, aren't you?" she said. "I suppose you are likely rather misunderstood. I know what that feels like, though in a slightly different way, you could say. I wish you could tell me your story — or your name, at the very least."

She smiled as the dog lay down, his huge dark head in her lap. His fur was nearly all black, with a white patch on his chest and brindle sprinkling his legs. Her writing complete for the moment, she set her notebook aside and leaned back against the tree, closing her eyes at the contentment of the dog and the sun, and she wished she could stay out here forever.

WILLIAM HIKED OVER HIS FIELD. He'd needed to feel the freedom of the outdoors after his morning. His headache had threatened to return, and he often found a brisk walk outdoors could keep it at bay. He'd left the house with his dog, but Friday had bounded off the moment they stepped outside. He whistled for him now, but the dog didn't come, which was rather unlike him. Usually Friday wanted nothing more than to follow his master. Ah well, he thought, he must have found something much more interesting to sniff or chase. William crested a hill, meandering his way toward the great oak. As a boy, he had climbed the tree so many times that his mother had stopped nagging at him to be careful and finally accepted that he would do as he pleased.

Now, in his adult years, he still found it a place of solace of some sort.

He stopped short when he looked down at the picture in front of him. His tree — and his dog — had been overtaken by a young woman. Rosalind leaned against the oak, her skirts fanned out around her and his dog draped over her lap. She looked the picture of contentment, in such contrast to the tense woman he knew.

He wasn't sure he wanted to speak to her again, to break the peace she had seemingly found, but all the same he was drawn toward her.

"Rosalind?" he said softly, not wanting to scare her, but

he seemed to do so just the same as she jumped. "My apologies, I did not mean to startle you."

"It's fine," she said with a slightly embarrassed laugh. "I seem to have become rather engrossed in my surroundings. I should be more attentive."

He waved his hand in the air. "No matter. It looks as if you have stolen the heart of my dog."

She smiled then, a real, beautiful smile he didn't think he had ever seen on her face before. It caused a dimple to form in her cheek, and she looked rather lovely, he thought, then shook his head. Where had these thoughts come from?

"He's wonderful," she said, and it was his turn to laugh. "I've never heard anyone but me say Friday is wonderful before." Apparently the dog had worked a spell over her.

"His name is Friday?" she asked, her eyes wide as she looked up at him.

"It is," he said, preparing for the usual question of how a dog had received so unusual of a name.

"Friday ... from *Robinson Crusoe*?" she asked, her nose wrinkled as though concerned she was going to be terribly wrong.

"Yes, exactly," he said, somewhat stunned. It was the first time someone had known the origin of the name. "You have read it recently, then?"

"Mmm, no, some time ago," she said, shaking her head. "I do love tales of adventure far beyond what I shall ever see in my life. I suppose that is what I love the most about a book — that it takes you places you never thought you could go to live out stories that would never be possible within one's own life."

He found himself captivated by her in that instant, by the way her face transformed as she looked out whimsically over the wild grasses of his lands. Somehow, despite her small frame and her plain though pretty face, she seemed like a different person here than the young girl he had known but had never really seen. He had always overlooked her, as she seemed to blend into the background. But that was not it, here, he realized. It was rather that she ... fit here.

"Have you read *Waverly*?" He asked. "It is a new tale, by Sir Walter Scott. You may enjoy it — I certainly did. I am sure it is somewhere in my library."

"I shall look for it," she said softly, and Friday's bulky body shoved up even closer to her, if that were possible. Rosalind smiled, reaching down a hand to absentmindedly scratch him between the ears, and the dog threw his head back in contentment.

"I believe I have something for you," he said, reaching into his pocket. He pulled out what Alfred had told him was her ring and necklace.

"Oh," she said, and he wasn't sure if he was imagining things, or if he saw a sheen of tears cover her eyes.

"I imagine you have been missing this," he said, holding out the wedding ring to her.

She took it from him, but instead of putting it on, she simply slipped it into her pocket and looked at the necklace instead.

"This was my grandmother's," she said, taking it from him and running her fingers over it somewhat lovingly. "But I thought it was broken?"

She looked up at him and William smiled. "I had it fixed."

Her words seemed to catch in her throat, and instead of speaking she reached behind her to return it round her neck. William watched her slim fingers work, until he noted she had attempted to do up the clasp a few times with no success.

"Allow me," he said, stepping behind her and taking the edges of the necklace in his fingers. He brushed the soft skin on the back of her neck and inhaled a fresh, sweet rosy scent from her hair as he did up the clasp. He had to snap himself out of his reverie to focus as he stepped back from her.

"Would you like to take a walk? See more of the land?" he asked, to which a smile of delight spread across her face. He reached down a hand to help her up, and when she took it, a strange jolt of heat spread through him from where her fingers touched his, something of a tremor to which he couldn't put a name or a cause.

"William, are you all right?" Her voice broke through his consciousness, and he realized he had been standing motionless for a moment, still holding onto her hand after she had used it to stand.

"Ah, yes, my apologies," he said, shaking his head and releasing her, smiling what he hoped looked to be a natural grin.

Their gazes locked, and his smile faded as he drank in her stare for a moment, her eyes reminding him of the shallow ocean, where the water turned green as it met the shore. As he thought it, he realized how silly he was being. He had only seen the ocean a few times as it were, and yet, she brought him back to those rare moments.

He held his arm out to her, and she took it with a smile, cocking her head toward him. He led her at a leisurely pace through the grasses, Friday following along at their heels, barking excitedly.

"Your property is beautiful," she said, her face turned out to the fields beyond them, leading to his woodland.

"Do you think so?" he asked, surprised. He had thought she would prefer the manicured gardens much more commonly found throughout the countryside. "My mother always felt they should be much more ... groomed, I suppose, however I haven't the heart to be rid of the gardener who refuses to tend to anything much beyond the courtyard."

"Most would likely feel that way," she said. "And yes, I do enjoy them as they are. Purposefully or not, you allow them to be free to be what they are meant to be, and not forced into what is expected of them, if that makes sense."

It didn't take much intelligence to realize that her views on the garden extended past that to her own life.

"Will you continue to wear the colors of half-morning through the party?" he asked her. "Not that you do not look lovely in them, but I can hardly imagine what it must be like to wear only black for an entire year, followed by the sombreness to which you now must wear."

He saw her eyes widen and, realizing how inappropriate his comment was, quickly tried to soften his words.

"Of course, though, you must miss your husband, and so it only makes sense to maintain an outward appearance. My apologies, Rosalind, I was being inconsiderate."

"Not at all," she said, shaking her head. "You are right. Black is rather dreary, and so are the grays. I don't mind lavender; however, I suppose I will have to come out of my half-mourning for the party as I only brought one or two dresses in these colors. It will give your guests something to speak of, I suppose."

"Do you really care so much?" he asked, studying her. "Why does it matter what they think?"

She stopped suddenly, and he had to step back to stay even with her. "I suppose ... I was raised to believe it always mattered. I hate the whispered gossip and veiled barbs that always seem to be on the lips of the *ton,* though what you say is absolutely right. It should not matter. It is my way of thinking that needs to change more than anything. It is difficult, however, to do so overnight."

"That is more than understandable," he said, smiling at her and the contemplation on her face.

"Oh, William, this is breathtaking!" she said, her eyes widening as she dropped her hand from his arm.

They had reached the small brook that ran through his property, just at the edge of the woodland. It was shallow, meandering, just enough of a water source to quench the thirst of the animals that lived in the woods beyond. He watched Rosalind gaze in rapt attention at the rabbits that hopped away from Friday, and the birds that soared overhead.

He hadn't seen his woods through another's eyes in some time, he realized, and suddenly felt fortunate at all that he was provided in this life. He realized that it was time he found someone to share it all with, and begin to grow a family who could enjoy it as much as he did.

"Rosalind," he asked, and she turned to face him, the smile lighting her face. "What are you running from?

9

Rosalind's breath caught. She wanted to enjoy this moment for what it was — a beautiful interlude in time within a setting that was as lovely as the man in front of her. She knew at some point he would ask her for more details of her situation, and she had been dreading the moment of explaining all to him, of bringing the ugliness of her life into his.

And yet, she found she couldn't keep from him the truth of all that happened. She looked down at her hands, then back at him, as he looked expectantly at her from eyes that showed true concern.

"The day of my husband's funeral, when you found me in the library..." she began, hesitating, not sure how much to tell him. She decided not to go into the details of her marriage. He didn't need to know how weak-willed she was that she had not escaped her marriage to Harold.

"Yes?" he said gently, encouraging her.

"I was upset for far more than my husband's death," she explained, her gaze on the ground. "You see, my brother-in-law, Bart, had just informed me of the lack of stipend available to me. My husband spent my dowry, and there are no available revenues for me."

"What?" he said incredulously, and she felt grateful for the anger bursting forth from him on her behalf. "That cannot be. 'Tis against the law!"

"I'm afraid not," she said, smiling ruefully. "Not if there truly isn't any revenue. It seems the estate was — and likely still is — in deep debt. Which is why it is rather ironic that your brother chose me to try to ransom." She gave a soft laugh. "No one cared or had the money for me."

"What of your parents?" he asked. "Surely they can provide for you."

"They could if they chose to," she said. "However, I am now four-and-twenty, and they had thought themselves rid of me. They feel I would be a burden upon my brother as he is now of age to marry. They preferred that I do what Bart wanted — marry him."

She saw his nose wrinkle in disgust.

"You know him, then?" she asked with a bitter laugh.

"I do," he responded. "And you have made the right choice to distance yourself from him. I am sorry, Rosalind."

"Yes, well," she said with a shrug, not wanting his pity. "I had a year, my mourning period, in which to find a way forward. I attempted many different tactics to look after myself, but none seem to have worked. Which is why I decided to throw myself upon the graces of Olivia and her husband, to see if they would take me for a time until I was able to ... sort out my situation."

"Do you mean to marry again?" he asked her, gently.

"No," she shook her head vehemently before she even realized what she was doing. "I will never marry again. I have found that one cannot trust that a man is who he says he is."

"You are speaking of your late husband, then."

She glanced over at him, at the compassion showing in his eyes, which were the color of the sky when night has just begun and there was still a bit of light remaining. "Yes," she said, unable to hide the truth. "Harold was a boor, and I am glad to be rid of him."

She saw him startle in surprise, and she was suddenly horrified by her words.

"I — I am sorry, William, I should not have said such a thing," she rushed on, feeling her cheeks flame. "Forgive me, and please, pretend I never said it?"

She looked up at him, hoping he could see the agony of her gaze, willing him to agree with her. She was shocked when he smiled at her.

"Why, Rosalind, I believe that is the first real emotion I have seen from you in some time — likely, in fact, since I found you pouring out your soul in the library of your husband's home."

"That," she said soberly, "was of frustration more than anything."

"I realize that now," he said, stopping to look at her, turning her to face him, his hand coming to her chin as he tilted her face up to him. "I would implore you, however, do not judge all men on Harold Branson. He was a true bastard, Rosalind, as is his brother. You are too precious a jewel to be lost forever on mistrust and unhappiness."

Her breath caught in her throat at his words. Why was he torturing her so? For hearing such words from his lips as he stared at her only made her want to believe that a man like this could actually feel something for her. She knew, however, it was only because of the moment they found themselves in and the pity he felt for her. He could never want a woman like her, not when there were vibrant, sensual women who would gladly become the wife he was looking for.

"You are too kind, my lord," she murmured. "But you are wrong. I am but a wallflower who was married for her dowry, not a woman that a man could love enough to provide me the happiness I am searching for."

"You are more than worthy," he said softly. "Do not think so little of yourself."

With that, he shocked her by bending his head and bringing his lips to hers in a kiss so tender, so gentle, she almost didn't realize what he was doing. How she had longed for a moment like this with a man like William — with William, himself, were she being honest. As she felt his hand come to the back of her head, his strong fingers sifting through the strands of her hair between her chignon and the sensitive skin underneath, a voice in her head told her that she was being fanciful, that she should push him away, so as not to let herself become hopeful that there was more than this available to her. And yet, she couldn't — she wanted this too much. She shut the pestering voice away and lost herself in the moment, feeling herself melt into him.

His left arm circled around her, and she felt herself pulled closer to him. She lifted her hands round his neck, and rather than simply enjoying herself, she gave back to him, pouring all of the emotions, all of the attraction that she had felt for him for years into the kiss. She didn't know how long their mouths moved over one another in a gentle rhythm, but eventually it was Friday who broke them apart. The dog, clearly feeling left out, pushed between them, and Rosalind had to laugh when his body began to shake with happiness at being between the people he had seemingly chosen as those he deemed important enough to bestow his affections.

Rosalind bit her lip, afraid for a moment to look at William, but finally bolstered her courage. When she met his gaze, however, it was not a look of amusement that stared down at her, but rather the look of a man suddenly tormented by feelings he wasn't sure what to do with. Perhaps, then, he had felt as much from the kiss as she had?

Unable to continue holding the intensity of his stare, Rosalind looked down, her hand coming to Friday's head. She didn't know what to say, how to respond. Harold had kissed her, sure, but it was never anything like this. Harold had kissed her as a means to get what he wanted, to please himself without any thought of her or what she may have felt. This kiss, however, had been equally, if not more, about her pleasure as well as William's.

She cleared her throat.

"Shall we return?" she asked softly, and William nodded tersely. Well, she thought, as they made their way back to the oak to gather her books and the quill and ink, was he to go back to the sour mood he had been in yesterday? She wasn't sure she could keep up with this. One moment he was the light, affable man she had always known, and the next he was short and quick-tempered. This was why one shouldn't give her heart away, Rosalind thought as she told herself to be careful, hesitantly taking his arm as they slowly walked up the hill, returning to the house in silence.

WILLIAM COULD HARDLY BELIEVE what he had done. He had kissed Rosalind, the woman his brother had abducted, who had been used as a pawn too many times in the games of others to trust anyone again. He had simply wanted to show her that she had worth, that she shouldn't hide herself away forever, and the next thing he had known she was in his arms and his lips were on hers. If Friday hadn't interrupted them, he wasn't sure how far he would have taken the kiss. It wasn't so much the action that had surprised him, however, but rather the emotion he had felt. She had touched something within him, and he wasn't sure if he was happy about it.

He hardly knew what to say to her now. Should he apologize? But how, when he felt as if she enjoyed it as much as he? Besides that, it wasn't as though she was a blushing debutante. She was a widow and understood the acts of love and the like. She certainly didn't seem as affected as he, however, as she kept the serene look on her face throughout their return to the house.

When they reached the doors leading inside, he bade her good afternoon and strode off to his study, determined that all he could do now was put space between himself and Rosalind, who seemed to be growing ever lovelier each time he saw her.

10

Later that evening, William pushed open the door to his library, looking for some solace. Fortunately, his headaches had stayed at bay throughout the day, though Alfred had not. His brother had pestered him, asking for one thing after another, and William sorely wanted to tell him to shove off. Instead, he took advantage of his brother's presence to have him help determine who the various items he had stolen belonged to. Even now, he had packages ready to be sent anonymously to various lords and ladies. Unfortunately, Alfred — and Richard, the bloody fool, who had not needed the money but rather enjoyed the thrill — had sold quite a bit of it already. At the very least, Alfred had not negated on his promise to stay away from Rosalind, for which William was grateful.

Rosalind. He had tried not to think of her throughout the course of the day, but she continued to enter his mind. His thoughts of her were also not the purest of sorts, for which he was sorry, although what he was to do about it, he wasn't sure. His house party was to start in a days' time, and by then he needed to have a grip on his emotions or he would make a fool of himself.

He could hardly believe that he had never noticed her before. Sure, she wasn't as striking nor as vibrant as Olivia. But there was something rather ... alluring about her. She had a peacefulness to her that drew him, that calmed him. No, she wasn't a tall, beautiful blonde. But her hair was the color of ... well, chocolate, he supposed, and when she smiled, her face lit up with a brightness that was hard to keep himself away from.

His footsteps across the room suddenly halted when he noted a presence in the corner of the room.

"Oh, William!" said the object of his thoughts, pushing herself into a seated position and then rising, as he had apparently startled her. "My apologies. I have availed myself of your wonderful library without invitation."

"It's fine," he said, waving her back down to her seat, as she had been curled into the corner of the brown French leather club sofa, a stack of books on the table at her elbow and a leather-bound volume he couldn't make out but recognized as having been with her that afternoon in her hands. "Have you found anything to which you have taken a fancy?"

"You have a wonderful selection," she said. "I am impressed. Why, you even have a Gothic novel or two!"

He laughed at that. "Let's keep that our little secret, shall we? But yes, I do enjoy a rather varied selection of books. I always have."

"As have I," she said with her true grin, the one that dimpled her cheek. "I enjoy most books really. As long as they do not end in sadness. I find there is enough grief in our world that if I am to read, I would prefer to immerse myself in a story that will bring me joy at the end of it."

He nodded. "I suppose you are right. Although some would say that it is better to come to terms with our reality."

She shrugged. "That may very well be, but I know enough of it. I am not naive, as some may think. I simply prefer to lose myself in worlds where all ends happily."

He realized suddenly she was speaking of her own situation, and he felt like a fool for bringing it to the forefront of her mind when clearly she had come here for a peaceful evening.

"You are not tired tonight?"

"Oh, no," she said with a wave of her hand. "I do not find I actually need that much sleep. In fact, most nights I stay awake reading before I fall asleep. Tonight I realized that I had already finished all I had brought with me and was looking for something new."

"Have you always enjoyed books?" he asked, interested suddenly in learning more about this woman with whom he had been acquainted for so long but realized he really didn't know at all. He took a seat in the chair across from her.

"Oh, yes," she said, a gleam coming to her green eyes. "Since I was a child, really. I have always loved losing myself in stories. It's a way to explore without leaving home, to learn to see the world through the eyes of others. One doesn't always agree with an author or a character, but it does open one's mind, does it not?"

He nodded contemplatively. "You are very perceptive, Rosalind."

Her cheeks turned pink and she looked down at the book in her lap, her long eyelashes hiding whatever emotion she may be feeling.

"Hardly," she responded. "Now, tell me, William, what has been your latest book of choice?"

It was his turn to feel his cheeks warm as he could not

immediately think of a title that a respectable gentleman should currently be reading. "Err — a novel recently published by a Thomas Egerton," he said.

"Oh! *Sense and Sensibility*?" she asked, her eyes lighting in recognition as well as a bit of mirth at his expense. "It is a lovely romance, is it not?"

"Yes," he said with what he knew was a sheepish grin. "That is yet another secret, however, Rosalind, that I shall have to ask you to keep to yourself."

"Very well," she said with a smile. "I promise to never reveal you to be the true romantic you seem to be."

He laughed then, pleased to see this side of her, the side that was witty, lighthearted, and fun. He had always seen her as the solemn, serious sort, but he realized now there was more to her, this other side that she kept hidden from most.

"What is that you have in your hands?" he asked, curious about what she was currently interested in.

"Oh," she said, covering the book as if hiding it would make him forget about it. "Nothing at all. Just a journal."

"Ah, you are writer too, then?" he asked, interested. "Recounting your own experiences?"

"I suppose you could say that," she said, suddenly shutting down, as if sharing more with him would render her more vulnerable than she cared to be.

"What do you write about?" he asked gently, probing, wanting to open her up, free the facade that so quickly shuttered back into place and hid her from him.

"Stories," she said, refusing to look at him, her face now a healthy pink, up to the roots of her hair.

"Of...?"

"People. Places. Relationships. Romance." Her short, staccato words came quickly, but only served to further intrigue him. He opened his mouth to ask more when there came a quick rap on the door.

"My lord," his butler said, entering the room, stopping when he realized Rosalind was there. "My apologies, I did not realize you were entertaining. However, my lord, you asked that I inform you when it was time, and ... it is time."

"Time for ... oh! Yes, wonderful, thank you McGregor. Rosalind, my apologies, but I must go."

"Is everything all right?" she asked, concern cloaking her face.

"Yes, absolutely. Well, I should hope so anyway."

"What is it?" she asked, and he hesitated. He really shouldn't speak of such things in front of a woman; however, he supposed she was no longer an innocent young lady....

"There is a dog having pups," he said, to which her eyes widened.

"You have more dogs?" she asked.

"Well, this one, she is actually my neighbor's dog. It seems she and Friday ... well, ah, are having young. The dog's taken a liking to my stable, and so that is where she has remained for the past few days. I asked the groom to keep an eye on her. I thought to ensure everything is all right when the birthing time came."

"Oh," she practically purred, her eyes like saucers now. "May I come with you?"

"Come with me? To a birthing?"

"Yes!" she said, showing more enthusiasm than he had ever seen from her. "Please?"

At that single word of entreaty, he sighed. He knew he shouldn't agree to this. And yet, she looked so eager that he did not have the heart to say no.

"Very well," he said finally. "Come."

The stable was not far from the house, and Rosalind

kept up with his quick pace. When he reached the stable door, he found a groom crouched over the dog, who was offering up pants and some whimpers.

"Is she all right?" Rosalind asked breathily, following him to the corner, where the dog lay on soft straw. They crouched beside her and the groom.

"I'm not sure," the man said. "I've helped birth horses before, but never dogs. She seems to be having a bit of difficulty. No pups have come yet."

William, having grown up in the country, had been witness to plenty of births and leaned down to see if he could assess what was the issue. Rosalind, meanwhile, walked around to the dog's head, lifting it and laying it in her lap, stroking the dog's soft fur while whispering gentle words in her ear.

"It's all right, darling, you're doing absolutely wonderful," she said softly, and William wondered if she had forgotten he and the groom were present, or if she really didn't care in the moment. "Soon, you will have birthed your puppies, and you will be a mother! How wonderful that will be."

William smiled for a moment, forgetting his ministrations. He looked at her, the gentle compassion and tenderness on her face, and he felt a strange twinge in his heart. Who was this enigma of a woman? His attention was brought back to the dog, and he found the problem, slowly turning the first pup within to help it come into the world. It slid out, and he caught the squirming bundle, to which Rosalind gasped in surprise and excitement. Four pups later, the mother was tending to her newborns, who he helped begin to suckle at their mother's side.

When William looked up, Rosalind had the most tender, loving look covering her face.

"Oh William," she said, wiping away a tear that fell down her cheek. "It is so absolutely beautiful."

He looked at her, at her lavender muslin skirts spread wide about her in the straw, her long, chocolate brown hair falling out of its usual chignon to wave about her shoulders, and he was captivated. *She* was the beauty here, which shone forth from the look of rapture upon her face as she looked at the animals around her.

William felt like a bit of a fool for not noticing her earlier. Yet there had always been Olivia. Though it was funny — he hadn't thought of Olivia in the past couple of days since Rosalind had arrived, despite the fact her presence should have reminded him of her friend, should it not have? No, Rosalind did not have Olivia's spunk, but she had something else, something he couldn't quite determine. And when he thought of Olivia now he felt ... nothing.

He walked to the corner of the stable and washed his hands in a pail of water. He returned to the dogs and extended his hand to Rosalind.

"Well, Rosalind, perhaps that is enough excitement for one evening?"

She took his hand, and he startled at the jolt the contact once again sent up his arm. When she stood, she was but inches away, and he slowed his breathing to try to still his racing heart.

"Would you mind if I visited them on the morrow?" she asked, still gazing in awe at the dogs, and he couldn't understand how she seemed so unaffected by their contact.

"Of course not," he finally said, shaking his head at his foolishness. "Come as often as you wish. Ah, Friday, you've decided to visit. Meet your children, boy."

He laughed as the dog meandered into the stable, and

he and Rosalind began making their way back toward the house.

Rosalind tilted her head back, and he followed her gaze up to the stars that shone down on them from the navy sky.

"Do you not think it's strange, William, the way we treat the children in our society?"

"What do you mean?" he asked, confused by her words.

"We birth children and then are supposed to provide for them in every way possible. We give them shelter, food, and, all they might require. And then we hire other women to look after them, to see to their every need," she said. "Does that not strike you as ... wrong, in some way? Does a child not want his or her mother and father more than any other? You see the way the animals are. As babies, they spend all of their time with their mothers. And yet we practically give our children away to another."

"I do not suppose I have every thought of it quite like that," he said, though her words did beg an interesting question, one he had never considered.

"Oh, I am being foolish," she said, waving a hand in the air with a nervous laugh. "Do not mind me. I suppose I am just being overly emotional."

He wondered if perhaps she had resigned herself to the fact she would spend her life alone, that she was mourning the loss of the opportunity to have children with her husband, or, perhaps, even reflecting on her own childhood. Whether it was a happy one, he wasn't sure, although she had always seemed content enough when she visited with Olivia's family. He didn't know what to say to her now, to ease her fears or her tension, and she seemed to sense the awkwardness that filled the air as much as he.

"Well, good night William," she said, a look of regret in

her eyes. “One more day until the house party, I suppose, is it not?”

“Yes,” he said, suddenly regretting that he had invited all of these people to stay at the house with the two of them. He enjoyed having her to himself. “One more day.”

She climbed the stairs, alone, and he wanted nothing more to follow her, but instead he sent his booted feet back toward the library.

11

Rosalind smiled as she looked at the tiny pups, squirming as they searched out their mother. She had not even stopped for breakfast before running out to the stable to see them. Friday had left his master's side to stand guard in front of his family, and she laid a quick kiss on his head before sitting down to provide her attention to the mother and the puppies. There were five of them, and she determined that they needed names, though she wasn't sure if she should be the one to provide them. That right should go to the owners, should it not?

She was tickling a puppy under the chin when the door of the stable slowly opened, and she looked up with a smile on her face, expecting William. Her smile slowly fell when the light silhouetted Alfred instead. He leaned against the doorjamb, taking her in with a look in his eye that made her shudder.

"Well, well, Lady Templeton," he drawled out slowly. "What a surprise, to find you here alone."

"Leave me be, Alfred," she muttered, angry that her current circumstances meant that this man should continue to be a part of her life when she wanted nothing more than to be rid of him forever.

"Ah, but you would like that, wouldn't you, darling?" he said, and she closed her eyes, willing him to leave. "However, you are a guest here at my family's home, and therefore have no right to make demands of me."

"You *kidnapped* me," she said angrily. It was true, she rather abhorred conflict, but she was also not willing to back down when she believed so strongly that she had been wronged.

"That I did," he said with a mock sigh. "Though you were not worth it at all."

She narrowed her eyes at him. "Do you expect me to apologize for that?

He laughed. "You have more backbone than I originally thought, Lady Templeton."

"Why will you not leave me alone?" she said, no longer caring that she showed him the exasperation she felt. "I want nothing more to do with you."

"So why have you not told anyone about me and what I did?" he asked, and her eyes dropped to her lap, as she didn't want to show him any inkling of what she was feeling. "Would it, perhaps, have anything to do with the fact that you would prefer no one know where you are?"

"What are you talking about?" she gritted out, unsure of what he knew of her situation.

"I know that your parents referred your ransom to your brother-in-law, Lord Templeton. I know that good ol' Bart had no money to pay your ransom. However, he was also rather interested in your whereabouts. I was holding out for a payment before I told him, but I certainly could, if I so chose."

"You wouldn't dare," she seethed.

"I would," he said, "if you were to do anything stupid, such as try to win my brother's affections. I cannot have you here, Lady Templeton. You are a constant reminder to my brother of my actions, and he already seems to want to be rid of me as it is. No, you have to go."

"I have been invited to the house party," she said, trying not to betray any emotion.

"You have," he said. "And I will give you a week before I send word to Lord Templeton. But in the meantime, you must realize that whatever flirtation you think you have with my brother is just that — a flirtation. You know, as well as I do, that he will always be in love with your best friend, Lady Olivia, though she is now, of course, the Duchess of Breckenridge. In fact, there is a delightful young woman coming to our house party, Lady Diana Watson, who I'm sure William will find rather lovely and so like your friend Lady Olivia. Her father is an earl; however the lady is somewhat outspoken, which has scared off many a gentlemen. Unless, of course, said gentleman appreciate such qualities."

He leaned back with a smirk. "Well, then. Good day, Lady Templeton."

As he walked off, she didn't want to admit that he had a point, but in truth he certainly did. William might be showing her attention at the moment, but there was nothing and no one else to currently distract him or occupy his thoughts. He had kissed her, true, but would he again, when he had other events and people capturing his attention? She wasn't sure.

Rosalind was trying to put thoughts of her time in the hunting cottage behind her, but it was difficult when she was constantly reminded by Alfred's presence. She had, however, chosen to remain here, so she would have to deal with him.

In truth, her ordeal in captivity could have been much worse. The men — Alfred and Richard, she now knew — had actually left her alone for the most part. It was her own fears that had been worse than anything. She had been afraid they would come back, force themselves on her, or be rid of her when their attempts at ransom proved futile. Fortunately, neither man seemed to have the stomach for anything so particularly vile.

She sat back now against the hard timber of the stall door, unable to hold back a smile as she watched the mother lick her pups with affection. Her parents had never allowed her to have dogs, and oh, how she loved them. They had a country home, of course, but her mother had hated it, finding it "ever so dull and dreary," and therefore even when her father was attending to business at their estate, Rosalind and her mother had often stayed in London. She hadn't realized how cloying the city was until she got out of it. Even at Harold's estate, as much as she had disliked it, she still felt a sense of freedom that she never found in the city.

Rosalind wondered what William was doing at the moment. She knew his affairs were no concern of hers and yet ... she couldn't keep him from occupying her thoughts. He had seemed to warm to her the past couple of days, despite his initial shortness with her. If only the house party could stay away, she thought with a sigh. But that was part of life, wasn't it? Embracing all the moments, even those you dreaded.

The stable door opened, and the man who had occupied her thoughts walked in, his boots shuffling through the straw.

"Rosalind!" he exclaimed upon coming across her on the floor of the stable, and she wondered whether she actually heard some pleasure in his voice, or if he was simply surprised to find her amongst the dogs.

"Hello, William," she said rising after moving the puppies off her lap to their place with their mother. "How are you this morning?"

"Just fine," he said. "I say, did I see Alfred leaving here?"

"You did," she sighed. "He came in for a ... visit."

"My apologies," he sighed, running a hand through his hair, leaving it tousled, and she felt an urge to reach her hand out to fix it, though she knew she never would actually do such a thing. "That must have been difficult. In truth, I am unsure exactly what to do in this situation. It is not one that is particularly ... common."

"It's fine," she said, not meeting his eye as she wasn't being entirely honest. "Are you here to see the dogs?"

"I am checking on them, yes, but I am actually fetching my horse as I must be on my way to visit a tenant," he responded.

"Oh, lovely. It is a rather beautiful day for a ride," she said wistfully.

"You ride, then?" he asked, a bit surprised, and she felt herself blush.

"Not well," she said. "I have not had much opportunity. When I have, though, it has been quite enjoyable."

"Come along then," he said with an impish grin, and her heart melted. Why must he be so charming?

"I likely shouldn't," she found herself saying despite the anticipation his words had brought her. "I would only slow you down."

"Ah, I am in no hurry," he said with a wave of his hand. "What do you say? I'll even have Cook pack a picnic lunch."

"A picnic? Oh, that is tempting," she said, wanting so badly to accompany him and yet knowing the closer she came to him, the more she would want what could never be hers.

"Say yes," he said, and she knew, deep in her heart, that she could never truly say no to him.

"I — all right then," she smiled. "When do we leave?"

ROSALIND WAS RIGHT ABOUT one thing, William realized. She could not ride very well. His stables weren't large, but he had saddled an older mare for her, one who actually wasn't ridden near often enough. She was a good fit for Rosalind, slow and steady, though William could practically see the horse rolling her eyes at Rosalind's feeble attempts to direct her one way or the next.

"With a little more force, Rosalind," he called over to her, trying to suppress his grin. "Let her know that you're in charge."

She nodded and tried again, but her heart wasn't in it, and eventually William rode ahead, while Rosalind's horse was content in simply following along behind. They took a very leisurely pace, but the tenant wasn't too far and soon they arrived at the small stone building, which had pens filled with animals out back. As they led their horses up the small lane, a group of young children ran out to greet them, calling out to William by name. While he had a steward, he enjoyed getting to know many of his tenants personally. He found his estate could be lonely at times, and he liked having the opportunity to converse with others.

"My lord!" A woman came out of the house, wiping her hands on a cloth. "Lovely to see you. I will find my husband for you. Children! Leave Lord Southam alone, please."

"Not a problem, Mary. I quite enjoy the children," he

said truthfully. He rarely had the opportunity to spend time with children. It was another reason he enjoyed these visits. He knelt down in front of them. "Now, let's see what we may find in my pockets. Hmmm. Oh look, sweets! Now, these wouldn't interest you, would they?"

The children shrieked and laughed, clambering for a piece of chocolate, and William laughed along with them. He looked up at Rosalind, who was standing over his shoulder with a wide grin on her face and a look in her eyes that he couldn't quite decipher.

"Ah, children, even more important than candy, however, is my guest. Meet Lady Templeton. She is staying at our manor and was very interested in coming to visit with you. Lady Templeton, this is Mary Baker."

"Welcome, Lady Templeton," said the woman, who had just returned, and gave her a quick curtsy. "We are honored to have you here."

"Oh, please, none of that," said Rosalind with an embarrassed wave of her hand. "And Rosalind is fine."

"Lady Rosalind," said Mary with an incline of her head, reaching out a hand to her husband, who had rounded the corner. "My husband, Tom."

William exchanged pleasantries with the man then followed him inside to discuss business dealings. He looked at Rosalind and she gave him a bit of a nod as if to say she was perfectly fine with being left alone with Mary and the children. He smiled at her and continued on.

THEIR BUSINESS CONCLUDED, William shook hands with Tom then went to find Rosalind. He looked around the front yard of the house, but finding no sight of her, he continued around back. He stopped short when he saw her in the distance. She had unpacked the picnic Cook had put together. And now she sat in the middle of the blue checkered blanket, the five children of various sizes sitting around her and Mary. They were laughing as they ate, and as he took them in, his heart swelled. Who was this woman? He knew she had been raised Rosalind Kennedy, the daughter of an earl, and yet she sat now in the middle of a field with one of his tenants and her multitude of children, not only sharing food but also stories and laughter. Here, she seemed more at ease than he had ever seen her before at an event held within Society.

Interesting, he thought, and he wasn't sure what to do with the feelings that were growing inside him when he looked toward her. Could she be the partner he was looking for? He needed a woman who would help him, who would be accepted by his peers and his people. He had always loved women with backbone, who would stand up for what they believed in. She wasn't that woman, but did he truly need that in a wife? He admired her, that was true, and he knew he could get along well with her. Was that not enough?

And yet she now did not exactly have the best history with his family, and he wasn't sure they could ever all live together in harmony. Was she more important than his mother and brother?

He didn't realize how long he had been standing there, until he heard Rosalind call out to him.

"Will— Lord Southam!" her voice rang out, and he began to approach them, taking in her rosy cheeks, mussed hair, and wide smile showing her perfect teeth. "I must apologize, but I have shared our picnic lunch. I hope you do not overly mind?"

"Mind? Of course not. As long as you little imps have saved me some of Cook's delicious scones!"

He grabbed a pastry and popped it in his mouth with a grin, to which the littlest of the children started laughing at him.

William watched Rosalind out of the corner of his eye as she smiled at the lot of them. What was he to do with her?

12

"Come on, girl, let's go," Rosalind tried her best to coax the horse along, but in truth the mare was a stubborn sort, and seemed determined to go along at her own pace. Rosalind sighed and decided to simply accept it. Neither she nor the mare would be winning races anytime soon, that was for certain. Ah, well, not that it mattered, she thought.

As they came closer to William's manor, Friday came running out to meet them.

"Hey there, boy!" William said with delight. "Leaving your family, are you? Well, we all need to stretch our legs now and then, do we not?

Rosalind laughed at the way he spoke to the dog, as if Friday was human and understood every word he said. Although, if she were being honest, she did the same. She supposed that one could truly judge the character of another by the way he treated an animal. And William, clearly, had a very worthy heart.

He was quite a hands-on lord, not one who entrusted most of the responsibilities to his steward. She found that rather admirable. In fact, there wasn't much about him that she didn't admire.

If only she was the type of woman that a man like him would want, she thought with a sigh. But no, she didn't fit with his life, nor his family, nor his idea of the perfect woman.

"'Tis rather warm for the season, is it not?" he asked her, cutting through her thoughts, and she smiled at the idle chatter he made with her.

"It is," she agreed. The sun *was* rather warm, and despite the light gown she wore, she felt a trickle of perspiration slide down her spine.

"I have an idea!" William said suddenly, and she caught the impish grin that spread out over his face, the type of smile she remembered from her visits with Olivia as children. Usually it meant he had found trouble, though the adult William had seemed to embrace the responsibilities he had inherited.

"Yes...?" she asked cautiously.

"How would you like to visit my favorite fishing hole?"

"A fishing hole?" she repeated.

"Yes," he said. "It's down the hill beyond those trees, to where the river runs. It offers plenty of shade and perhaps we could even dip our toes in the water, if you're up for it."

"I suppose," she said with a shrug and a smile. It did sound rather lovely.

As he had told her, it wasn't far, and she was rather awestruck when they broke through the trees to the lovely little spot.

"I told you that this was my favorite fishing hole," William said, dismounting and coming over to give her a hand down. "I suppose I should have mentioned it was my only fishing hole as well."

He laughed then, a rich, warm chuckle that was contagious, and Rosalind found herself laughing along with him.

"Do you fish often?" she asked him.

"I do," he replied with a nod. "Though to be honest, it isn't so much the fishing that draws me as the peacefulness. No one usually knows I'm out here. My brother never comes here, my steward cannot find me ... it's rather lovely."

"You usually come alone then?" she asked, moving to stand beside him as they looked out over the water.

"I do," he said, turning to her with a smile. "But with you, I know the peace will not be broken. There is something about you, Rosalind, that makes me feel ... comfortable. I do not have to pretend, nor put on a show for you. I enjoy that."

Rosalind dipped her head, embarrassed by his words. She supposed it was a compliment, but she wasn't entirely sure how to respond.

"Thank you, William," she finally murmured.

"Now, come!" he said, breaking the silence and walking to the shallow water. He sat down on the edge, took off his shoes, and began rolling up the legs of his trousers. Rosalind simply watched as he lowered his feet into the water, leaned his head back, closed his eyes, and basked in the sun on his face. She swallowed hard, even though he had simply removed his stockings.

"Is the water cold?" she asked.

"Not at all," he said, keeping his eyes closed, now lying backward in the long grass. "If you wanted to try it yourself, I promise I will not look."

She laughed. "I would not want to entice you with a view of my ankles, my lord."

She colored suddenly, realizing what she had said. "That is—"

"I can assure you, Rosalind, that the sight of your ankles will do nothing to change my opinion of you."

Rosalind slowly walked toward him, taking a seat beside him. She took off her shoes as he had, and reached up under her dress to roll down her stockings. He was true to his word, and did not lift an eyelid.

When she finally slid her feet into the water, she realized he was right. It *was* rather glorious. She lay back beside him, closed her eyes herself, and soon enough found that between the calm of the air, the soft flow of the water, and the sun on her skin, she was lulled to sleep.

WILLIAM SMILED as he watched the peace take over Rosalind's face. She was always so tense, so concerned with everything going on around her. For once, she had allowed herself to simply feel, and when she let go of all that worry, she was truly beautiful, he realized.

She woke some time later, when William was still contentedly lying on the bank.

"Oh!" he heard her exclaim, as she rose to a seated position. "Was I *asleep*?"

"You were."

"For how long?"

"Not long. Half an hour or so?"

"My goodness!" she said. "I never sleep."

"What do you mean, you never sleep?" he asked, perplexed. "Everyone sleeps."

"Well, I do sleep, but I do not sleep many hours, and I *never* sleep during the day." She looked so vexed that he wanted to laugh, but he realized that she was being entirely serious and therefore kept his mirth at bay.

"Sleeping during the day, I must tell you, is rather wonderful," he said with a smile.

She rose to her feet suddenly, brushing her hands on her skirts. As she did so, she accidentally kicked one of her boots into the water. "Oh no!" she said, kneeling in the grass as she desperately made to retrieve it before it sank to the bottom of the pond. Her action must have put her off balance, for before William could react, she tumbled into the pond with a yelp.

Before he could think the situation through, William jumped in after her. It was only when his feet suddenly hit the bottom with a thud that he realized there had been no need — the pond came only up to his waist.

"William!" came her cry, partly in anguish and partly ... laughter?

He looked down at her where she sat in the water. Her hair had come loose and was trailing around her shoulders, but perhaps not in the most becoming way. It was sopping wet, hanging limply around her face. She pushed back a soaked lock from her eyes so she could see better. She looked around, at her gray skirts floating around her, and at William standing beside her.

She lifted her face and gave him an incredulous look.

Their eyes locked, and before they could help themselves, they both dissolved into laughter.

"What were you thinking?" she finally managed.

"I thought perhaps you couldn't swim!" he said with a shrug.

"I cannot," she said with a grin. "But I can walk."

"I somehow forgot how shallow this part of the pond was," he said with a rueful shrug. "You must admit, however, that the water feels rather fine, does it not?"

"It does," she nodded.

"Now, come," he said moving toward her and wrapping an arm around her waist to steady her and help her stand. "At the very least, allow me to help you to the bank. You must give me the satisfaction of doing *something* to feel like a gentleman here to rescue you."

"Very well," she agreed, and placed a hand on his chest to brace herself. She looked up at him, her mouth open as if to say something, but suddenly his breath caught in his throat. She was so very near, her face just inches from his. Her lips slowly came together, her words lost, and they stared at one another, drinking each other in. He wasn't sure which one of them moved first, but suddenly their lips were locked tightly together. Everything else seemed to disappear, and soon she was not just standing in front of him, but had her arms wrapped tightly around him, pulling him in closer as if she could hardly get enough of him. He understood, for he felt the same. Her lips were soft under his, her body, though sopping wet, warm and pliant. She leaned in to him, and he groaned as his manhood strained against the tight fabric of his pants. He had never made love in the water, he thought, and then tried to push the idea out of his mind as quickly as it had entered it. This was a lady, for goodness sake — he was not going to take her in the middle of his fishing hole!

Nor take her at all, he told himself. She was a widow, true, but he knew enough of her to understand that she not that kind of woman.

Yet, still, he could not stop himself from wanting more of her. He reached his hand behind her back to loosen the tight, wet laces, and then let the dress fall from her shoulders. His hands moved of their own accord, roving over her soft skin. He groaned into her mouth, his tongue finding hers and beginning a love play that coaxed forward a moan from her as well.

She was so small, so slender, and yet when his hands found her breasts, he reveled in the shape of them, the small, soft mounds that were so lovely. He rubbed her nipples through the thin fabric of her chemise, and she leaned further into him, nearly breaking all the self-control he had managed to hold on to thus far.

"William," she murmured, and it was enough to make him realize that if he didn't pull back now, before it went any further, he wasn't sure if he ever could.

He lifted his head from hers, hearing their rapid breath mingle, and he raised a hand to push back a lock of damp hair from her eye.

She looked at him then, full on in the eye, and he wondered how he had ever overlooked this woman, who wore all her emotion in the storm of her sea green eyes. She didn't say much, no, but then when she did speak, it always meant something, and left him wanting more.

He let his forehead rest on hers as they came back to the moment. They stood there, arms still around one another standing in the waist-deep water of the pond, with only the song of nature around them breaking through the silence. It wasn't until Friday gave a bark, as if he were tired of waiting for them to come out of their reverie, that William finally lowered his hands and stepped back from her.

He gave Rosalind what he hoped was a convincing smile then said, "Come, let us get you back to the house and into some dry clothing."

He reached out a hand and led her back to the bank, climbing out himself before crouching and lifting her out. She didn't weigh much, true, but her skirts were heavy as soaked through as they were.

"Oof," he said, when she came out of the water with more force than he had anticipated, and he found himself on his back gazing up at her. She looked at him, then down at herself in all of her dishevelment, and she let out a tinkling laugh once more. This time, she helped him up, and he suggested they walk their horses back to the house. He figured it might be a bit more comfortable for her.

Rosalind readily agreed, and as they slowly returned, she teased him a bit. Between that and the little glances she stole when she thought he wasn't looking, he was overcome with a sense of contentment that he had not felt in a very, very long time.

13

"Southam, my good man!"

Rosalind snapped her book shut as she heard a voice echo down the long corridor which extended from the front vestibule and into the library, which occupied the southeast corner of the house. She had become used to spending much of her time in this room. It was comfortable, with its dark wood and rich colors. She had also come to enjoy the fact that William spent a great deal of time here himself. He had his own small office upstairs, but he seemed to prefer this room. This corner had, through unspoken agreement, become hers, while William preferred the chair across from it.

While they found themselves often in deep conversation, they had also become comfortable in companionable silence, Rosalind with her books or her journal. She had written quite a lot since she had found herself a guest of William Elliot's. Not an invited guest, true, but they had seemed to find an ease with one another, and she dreaded the fact that she would soon have to leave.

She had been equally uneasy about the house party, but it was not as if she had any say in the matter as plans for it had been well underway before her arrival and it, in fact, provided her a reason to stay.

She should be pleased about it for William, she told herself. He had always been a man who thrived on being part of a social gathering, and she should be happy he was having this opportunity to spend time with his acquaintances and enjoy himself.

It was difficult, however, when she knew the underlying purpose of the party — to find William a wife. Lady Southam hadn't actually said it, but had continued to imply it often enough, although with an underlying message that Rosalind was not considered a candidate. Rosalind did her best to avoid the woman, but when she did find herself in the same room, as she had at breakfast that morning, Lady Southam had talked on and on quite animatedly about the many beautiful young ladies who would be arriving over the next day, and how fortunate it was that William would have the opportunity to meet them before, hopefully, any of the other young gentlemen.

As Rosalind's stomach had turned, she had found herself having to make a concerted effort to force down the rest of her breakfast.

Now, she heard William greet the new arrival, but it did not sound to be the arrival of a young lady, as Lady Southam had so hoped.

"Lord Merryweather!" she heard William call out in greeting, and she smiled slightly. She had, of course, met Lord Merryweather on many previous occasions, and he had always seemed to be a pleasant sort of man. She was pleased he was one of the house party attendees. In fact, she didn't know for certain who all would be arriving. She had yearned to ask, but knew it was not particularly polite to do so.

She heard the two talk spiritedly, and Rosalind returned to her book, although she found she could no longer become engrossed in it as she previously had been. She was now too distracted. She piled her books in her hands, deciding she would take them to her own, quiet room for the remainder of the day.

She was making her way down the corridor to the staircase when she heard a peal of laughter from the entrance hall beyond. She stopped still, frozen. She recognized that laughter. She had heard it far too often, and it usually did not bode glad tidings.

Rosalind shook her head, clearing it, trying not to let this affect her. She did, however, quicken her pace to the stairwell, trying to reach it before the woman saw her. Almost there, she thought, and had one foot on the bottom step when she heard a voice cry out her name and she groaned inwardly.

"Do tell me that is not Lady Templeton?"

Rosalind took a deep breath and turned.

"Lady Hester Montgomery," Rosalind said with a forced smile. "How lovely to see you."

"And you as well," said Hester, a cat-like smile forming on her lips.

It was certainly *not* lovely to see Lady Hester. She looked the same as she always had, her dark hair piled on her head over a pale face and ruby lips. She had the look of a doll, and yet the soul of a nasty witch. She had tried her best to ruin Olivia prior to her marriage, and then destroy it once she was happy. Olivia had forgiven her, but Rosalind had never forgotten the woman's actions. Hester's friend, Lady Frances Davenport, was close behind her, as always, though said nothing but simply nodded at Rosalind.

Of all the women in England, did the two of them really have to be in attendance?

"Ah, I see you are acquainted," said William, walking up to them, his arms behind his back, a look of concern passing over his face.

Of course William knew they were acquainted, thought Rosalind. Did he not know how much Olivia despised the woman?

"We are," said Hester, looking up at him with a coy smile. "I had no idea you would be here, however, Lady Templeton, being a new widow and all. Is it not slightly ... unfashionable to be in attendance at a house party so soon? You would not want people to have the wrong impression of your sentiments toward your late husband, now would you?"

Anger simmered in Rosalind's belly, but she kept an outward calm. It was moments like this that she wished she had Olivia's wit and disregard for what anyone might think, but no, she instead became dim-witted, her thoughts jumbled as she was unsure of exactly what to say.

"It has been over a year since my husband passed," she finally said, though why she felt the need to defend herself, she wasn't sure. "And, in any case, I was simply passing through and Wil— Lord Southam was kind enough to invite me to stay on for the house party."

"I see," Hester said, raising an eyebrow, clearly seeing more than Rosalind had intended. "You are as studious as ever, are you not, Lady Templeton? That is quite the pile of books you carry. An interesting pastime for a house party."

Rosalind felt her face grow warm.

"Yes, Lord Southam has quite a deep library that he has been generous enough to allow me to avail myself of."

"Well how kind of him. Do not let us keep you. Your arms must be simply aching!" With a gleam in her eye, Hester turned, placed her arm on William's, and looked back over her shoulder at Rosalind with a smirk on her face.

Steeling her heart, Rosalind turned and practically raced to her room before William could say a word.

By dinner that evening, all of the guests had arrived. Rosalind had spent most of the day within her own chambers, not wanting to have to make appropriate, painful, conversation with each arriving guest. If she was being truthful, she was also hiding from Hester Montgomery. She had never had to face the woman on her own, but had always had a friend at her side. This time was quite different.

Rosalind looked through the meagre assortment of dresses she had brought with her, unsure of what she should wear. Could she wear color? Or should she settle for a lavender, the gray now near ruin from the pond. Would one be sending the wrong message, as Hester had suggested? She had finally decided on the pale lavender that was somewhat fashionable while still following the procedures of half-mourning.

She had laid it across the bed when she heard a soft scratch on the door. She opened it to find a young maid standing outside of it with a smile on her face. "Good evening, my lady," she said. "Lord Southam requested that I make myself available to you, as your lady's maid was unable to accompany you on your journey."

"Oh, thank you," said Rosalind. "Though I am sure you are quite busy with other responsibilities regarding the house party. I can manage on my own."

She made to close the door, but the maid didn't move.

"My apologies, my lady, but Lord Southam insisted. He said you would decline but I was to not take no for an answer." The girl chewed at her bottom lip, seemingly uncertain of how to continue, and Rosalind took pity on her and opened the door to let her in.

"And what would your name be?" she asked her.

"Patty, my lady," said the girl as she tucked a stray blonde ringlet back up under her cap.

"Well I must thank you, Patty," Rosalind said with a soft smile as she took a seat on the bed. "I am sure that you will make preparing for the festivities quite easier and more enjoyable for me."

"I do hope so," said the girl with an eager grin. "I must confess that I have never been a lady's maid before, though in my employment previous to this I was trained in all of the responsibilities in case I was ever needed."

"Well, then, Patty, I hope I shall be worthy as the first lady you will have served," said Rosalind with a bit of a laugh. "I suppose we best get started."

It quickly became apparent that while Patty was certainly not experienced in the role of lady's maid, she was enthusiastic, and with some guidance, Rosalind was soon dressed in her simple gown, her usual chignon slightly more styled with Patty's ministrations. Rosalind had been a bit apprehensive when the maid approached with the curling iron, but she managed to keep from flinching as the girl fixed a few curls around her temple. Rosalind hadn't the heart to tell her that her stubbornly straight hair would soon be limp locks around her face as the curl wouldn't hold for long.

When she joined the party in the drawing room, she was somewhat surprised at the number of people who had arrived. Lord Merryweather instantly greeted her, as cheerfully polite as ever. Alfred leered at her before adopting a smile when his brother gave him a bit of a glare. She determinately ignored him and his stubborn friend who refused to leave, Richard Abbottsford.

Rosalind was surprised to find there were two younger married couples taking part in the party, including Lord Benjamin Harrington and his wife, Lady Sophie. Rosalind had met Lord Benjamin in the past, and had always thought him to be somewhat of a rogue, but his wife seemed rather lovely and it appeared that he was rather settled now. There was also the Duke and Duchess of Barre, with whom Rosalind had not yet become acquainted.

Then there were the young women. Of course Lady Hester and Lady Frances were dressed in their finest, Hester doing all she could to receive the attention of the eligible young men. Lady Hester's mother was in attendance as her chaperone, as were the parents of Lady Frances. There was a beautiful young blonde woman, Lady Diana Watson and her parents, Lord and Lady Huntington, and Rosalind was delighted that Olivia's sister-in-law, Lady Anne Finchley, was in attendance with her mother.

Rosalind was looking around the room, somewhat overwhelmed, when William appeared at her elbow.

"Quite the crowd, is it not?" he asked, and the back of her neck tingled where his breath touched it while she felt an odd patter to her heart that he had chosen to speak to her when there were so many others who wished for the company of their host.

"It is," she agreed, trying to ignore some of the stares of curiosity. She realized that there may be some questions as to why she was here at this particular house party when she had not been amongst Society for some time, and her being only so recently out of her full mourning period. In fact, Hester had been correct, though she was being malicious — it was rather early for her to be in attendance at a full house party, but there was nothing she could currently do about the situation.

"I must say..." she said, knowing it was impolite to ask but she had to know nonetheless. "I find it slightly curious that you have invited Lady Hester Montgomery. Are you well acquainted with her?"

William turned his brilliant grin to her. "You seem to me a loyal friend, Lady Templeton, and therefore I am assuming that you feel the same disregard toward her as Olivia?"

"I do," Rosalind agreed with a nod. "Perhaps even more so."

He chuckled at that. "Yes, Olivia has told me in great detail how she feels about the woman on more than one occasion. Our mothers are friends, you see. In fact, most of the people present are here due to their connection with my mother, with a few exceptions."

"Where do you put them all?" she asked in a bit of amazement. This was a spacious house, to be sure, but she didn't know there were so many bedrooms.

"Lord and Lady Harrington live not far down the road, so they will be staying in their own home, attending some of the festivities of their choosing. Otherwise, we have ample accommodations."

She nodded, and was about to ask further questions of the activities to come the following days — she liked to be prepared — but as she opened her mouth, William's attention was commanded by Lord Huntington, and she found herself dismissed with a quick, "excuse me."

No matter, she thought, and went off to find Lady Anne.

14

"And then she what? By God, you don't say!" Alfred chortled at a story being told by Abbottsford as he lit a cheroot. The ladies had retired to the drawing room, and William sat back in his chair, taking a sip of his port and listening to the conversation around him. Abbottsford was well experienced in the events of Tattersall's, and was regaling them all with tales of his prized horse's latest feats.

It had been a lively dinner, and William felt like himself again, settled amongst his peers and friends of his mother. It had been some time since they had hosted a house party, but when another London season had passed without him securing a bride, his mother had told him in no uncertain terms that she was hosting a house party and would be inviting the perfect woman for him. If he did not further the acquaintance with at least a proposal of courtship, she told him, he was a fool.

He could see why his mother had thought Lady Diana Watson, daughter of Lord Huntington, was a woman he would be interested in. She was, if he were being honest, rather like Olivia, although slightly more polished. She laughed heartily, yet appropriately, and she had quick wit and wasn't afraid to say what was on her mind. She was everything he had ever thought he had wanted in a woman — until recently.

Throughout the dinner, he had continued to find his eyes straying to Rosalind. She had been quiet, subdued, unlike the woman he had come to know over the past few days. Oh, she made polite conversation with her table companions. She had spoken at length with the Duke and Duchess of Barre, seemingly getting on quite well with the pair of them, who wore the love and affection they had for one another rather openly. He knew his mother disapproved, but William was rather pleased to see that it was possible to have such continued emotion for one another.

Rosalind spent the rest of her time speaking with Lady Anne, a woman with whom she had become acquainted through Olivia. He wished she would do her best to meet others. He hosted enough parties that he was hoping to find a woman who could move as easily amongst his peers as did he.

His attention returned to the men around the table when he heard his name.

"Southam, tell me, is this little gathering not a farce to find a wife for yourself?" asked Merryweather, and most of the eyes turned toward him. "Are there any women to your liking so far?"

"Why, Merryweather, are you looking to find one for yourself?" William answered with a laugh, deflecting the question. "My mother has organized this party, gentlemen, although I am pleased that you were all able to attend," he said, aware that two of the men round the table were the fathers of said women in attendance. "I am appreciative of the many admirable qualities of all of the young ladies amongst us, and should any of them be interested in a mere viscount, I would be ever so flattered."

"I have heard it said that Lady Templeton has been in residence for a time," said Lord Huntington, startling William. Could no one keep their mouths shut? Although, judging from Alfred's knowing look toward Richard Abbottsford, he realized that the culprit was likely none other than his own brother, the man who had brought the woman here against her will. Except, it was not as though William was going to tell the men that particular story, now was he?

"Lady Templeton was passing through when her travel plans were suddenly interrupted," he said. "Therefore, I invited her to stay for the house party. As you may be aware, I have known her since I was a child through her friendship with the Duchess of Breckenridge."

He saw relief in the eyes of Lord Huntington. Clearly the desire for a match between William and his daughter was not only formed in the eyes of William's mother, but in the young lady's parents as well.

What was he to do now?

IF SHE HAD to hear one more piece of the latest contrived, untrue gossip of the *ton*, Rosalind thought she might walk over and hit the smug smile off of Hester's face. And yet Hester maintained the rapt audience of many of the ladies around the drawing room, so apparently she knew what she was doing.

Rosalind tried not to listen, and instead waited for the chime of the clock to determine how much longer it would be until she could escape to her own rooms. She was, however, beginning to realize that one of the positive aspects of being a widow was to no longer require the constant presence of a nagging mother or chaperone who told her when and with whom she should be speaking and that no, she could not retire early, nor leave a party to withdraw into other quarters.

She felt rather sorry for the young women who still required such direction, although she had to say that the mother of Lady Anne was rather a lovely sort, unlike Rosalind's own mother who had constantly harped on her for one reason or another. Even in this moment, Rosalind could practically hear her mother's voice in her ear, telling her to sit up straighter, to converse politely with the other ladies present, and to remove the perpetual frown off of her face.

It was not Rosalind's fault, however, that her face looked like that, she had told her mother on more than one occasion. It was simply the way her face was.

"Then, for God's sake, smile, Rosalind!" her mother would say, to which Rosalind would simply roll her eyes. It wasn't quite as easy as her mother made it out to be.

Hester launched into another tale, and Rosalind sighed as she looked around the room, pretty with it's blue-striped wallpaper, the color of a robin's egg. As lovely as her surroundings, however, she couldn't take much more of this. And then, she realized, as she thought of her mother, that she didn't have to take any more of it. No one was forcing her to be here. She was a widow now. A destitute one, true, but she had broken free of her mother's will. There was no need to continue here when that was the very last thing she wanted to be doing. Rosalind began rising from the low, curved-back chair with brass inlays, but then the door opened and the gentlemen returned. Her eyes found William and she promptly sat back down. It would seem at the moment that her body was more in tune with her heart than her mind.

"William!" His mother rose and greeted him with a kiss on the cheek, as if she had not seen him in days instead of just over an hour. "Darling, shall we not have some music and perhaps a bit of dancing? Do you not think that would be simply lovely?"

Rosalind didn't think so. She was a horrific dancer, and avoided it at all costs. She had learned the steps to the most popular dances tolerably enough from the multitude of dance tutors in her youth, but any man who partnered her soon became aware of her lack of skill.

"Oh, how lovely!" said the Duchess of Barre from beside her. "I love a good dance, do you not, Lady Templeton?"

Rosalind made a bit of a strangled sound, one that neither agreed or disagreed with the woman, and took a large, rather unladylike gulp of her wine. Anne, an accomplished piano player, was happy to begin the evening with music, and Rosalind tried to slink back in her chair to blend in with her surroundings.

She had never been a true wallflower, despite her very best efforts. Between her mother's pushing, her dowry, and her friendship with Olivia, she had always been asked to dance, though she knew it was never for her own company or conversation.

Rather, she was always just, well, there. She knew she was a pleasant enough woman, one who was agreeable to spend time with while a gentleman waited to dance once more with whichever woman had captured his attention.

Rosalind looked up, her eyes latching onto William as he walked toward her. He looked rather striking this evening.

Of course, he always did. The attention of most of the women in the room was trained on him, and yet he was making his way over to her. Rosalind's heart began beating rather quickly, and she couldn't make up her mind as to whether or not she wanted him to ask her to dance. She did not particularly want to perform in front of these people, and yet she wasn't sure she could watch him dance with anyone else, and she so longed to be in his arms.

The decision was taken away from her, however, when his mother stepped into his path. "William," she said, her voice trilling through the air. "Lady Huntington tells me that her daughter simply loves this song. Perhaps you would accompany Lady Diana in this set?"

The young blonde woman rolled her eyes at her mother, but smiled prettily for William who, of course, had no choice but to lead her into the middle of the room and begin the set.

A few other couples joined in, and it seemed as if the evening's festivities were well underway. Rosalind tried to focus her attention elsewhere, but her gaze kept drifting back to William and Diana. He was laughing at something she said, his head dipping toward her as he looked down at her while she animatedly chattered away to him.

"They look well together, do they not?" Rosalind turned to find Alfred leaning over her chair, his voice low in her ear.

"They do," she said with a shrug, feigning nonchalance.

"Come, come, Lady Templeton, if nothing else you can be honest with me after all we've been through together, can you not?" he said, his voice low in her ear. His breath rankled her, but Rosalind was determined not to let him see that his words were having any effect on her. "I do hope you weren't getting your hopes up that dear old William actually saw anything in you. You know as well as I do that he's spent his life hopelessly in love with Olivia. Now that she's married, well, he'll find one just like her. I think Lady Diana will do — at least, Mother thinks so."

Rosalind simply nodded and smiled, as her mother had taught her to do in any situation in which she did not have an answer. And to this, she truly did not. For the worst part about what Alfred said was that it was true. She knew as well as any what William's feelings had always been for Olivia, and Diana was rather like her. In fact, Rosalind could not fault Diana at all. She seemed a truly lovely girl, and would make a fine wife for William.

She allowed nearly the rest of the set to complete before she rose, and did what she had been longing to do all night — she left.

15

"I thought I'd find you in here."

William had been disappointed, but not entirely surprised, when he had seen Rosalind rise and leave the room before his dance with Lady Diana had come to an end. She had been so stealthy, he didn't think anyone else had noticed — except perhaps Alfred, who looked after her with a grin on his face that worried William.

It hadn't been difficult to ascertain where she had gone. In the few short days since her arrival, she had noted a particular fondness for the conservatory — nearly as much as the library. The room adjoined the drawing room, but it was at the other end of it, within the plants, where he found her curled up in a window seat with her forehead on the glass of the window, her breath leaving a fog upon it.

She didn't turn to look at him, but leaned back slightly from the window, her face now a reflection on the panes in the dark of the night.

"You needn't have come after me," she said. "You have your guests to see to."

"And you, Rosalind, are one of those guests," he said,

coming to stand behind her. "The one whose feelings I care most about."

She dipped her head then, still not turning around.

"I am simply not one for parties, I'm afraid," she said. "But that does not mean that you shouldn't enjoy yourself."

"I am finding it difficult to be happy, knowing you are not similarly so," he said. "What ails you? My dance with Lady Diana? I would have preferred dancing with you."

As he sat beside her, he caught the slight flush on her cheeks from the side. He leaned back slightly so that the profile of her face was in his view.

"You do not have to say such things to me," she said, long eyelashes hiding her eyes from him. "Lady Diana is lovely and a very fine dancer."

"So are you," he said, to which she gave a rueful chuckle.

"Clearly you do not recall ever dancing with me," she said lowly.

"No," he said. "Though I wish my memory was better, for I should like to know what it is like. Come," he said, standing and holding out a hand.

"I'd rather not," she said, shaking her head. "We likely should not return together and begin a dance."

"No," he said, a slow smile breaking out over his face as he looked down at her. "I was not suggesting we return. Give me your hand — trust me."

She looked up at him then, and without hesitation, put her hand in his. He led her around the bench and into the middle of the room. Strains of Anne's melody on the pianoforte reached them, and he drew Rosalind into his arms.

"May I have this dance?" he asked, and he saw her lips part in surprise.

"Someone may see us."

"We shall remain hidden from view. Now, Rosalind, I will ask you again — will you dance with me?"

"I will."

He gathered her close in his arms — much closer than would ever be proper in any English ballroom — and began to move back and forth with her. It was not a dance that required steps or etiquette, but a simple sway back and forth. William saw Rosalind close her eyes as she relaxed in his arms.

He lowered his lips to her ear. "Do not run," he said. "When you feel alone, or not at ease, tell me? Wait for me, and I will be there with you."

"Oh, William," she said with a bit of a tremor in her voice. "You are so kind to me but I — I feel as though I am not the woman for you. You enjoy social events such as these, balls and house parties and the like, and I would rather be alone with a book or a close friend or two. Do you not think that perhaps, before we find ourselves traveled so far down a road that we can no longer find our way back, we should go our separate ways?"

William stepped back from her. At first he was angry at her refusal of his affections, but then he took in the sorrow of her eyes and realized how much it pained her to say what she had.

"Do not be ridiculous," he said, although he inwardly had to acknowledge the truth to her words. A life with him was one which required social niceties, whether it be with others of the *ton* or his own people on his estate.

She opened her mouth to say more, but he no longer wanted to hear any more reasons as to why they should keep their distance. Before she could utter a word, he took her lips with his, halting whatever she was going to say with a searing kiss. His lips and his tongue explored hers, finding the velvet corners of her mouth as they locked in a firm embrace, his arms coming even more tightly around her and pulling her in close.

For a woman who said she preferred the quiet of solitude and claimed to be rather subdued, she certainly had a fiery passion to her. William groaned as he longed to take things further, to walk her over to the window seat and truly show her the depths of his feelings, but realizing where they were and who was in the house, he gently eased back from her, finishing the kiss with a soft peck on her lips followed by one on her forehead.

He held her close for a moment, continuing their rocking motion, before he leaned down and looked her in the eyes, his gaze holding hers.

"I must return," he said. "I would like you to do the same. Come back, will you?"

She said nothing, but he gave her one last soft kiss before striding out of the room and through the doors leading back to the drawing room. He hoped she would overcome whatever it was holding her back, he thought. *Come with me, Rosalind.*

ROSALIND PRESSED a hand to her lips as she could still feel William lingering there. She could scarcely believe he had come after her. Men never came after her. Never. Not like in the stories she wrote, in which the men arrived at simply the perfect time to make amends or to come to the rescue of their heroine. Why was William so different?

And what was it that had caused William to suddenly notice her, after all this time? She had known him for years. Not well, to be sure, but well enough that were he to have any sort of interest in her, she should have certainly caught his attention prior to now. She frowned. She was being too hard on him, she thought. She should be grateful for all he had done for her.

It did, however, somewhat bother her, the way people could so easily change. Harold certainly had. When she had met him, he had been a nice enough man who she had thought would make a fine husband, though she had realized early on he would never be a man who would entirely capture her heart. But then, once they had married, he had become someone she didn't even recognize — a monster, to be honest. She had been so thankful when he had turned from their bed back to his brothels.

She was no longer sure of her own judge of character. Could she trust William?

Rosalind rose and slowly made her way through the beautiful flowers and greenery of the conservatory, which was lit by the stars of the night sky through the windows, and leaned against the doorjamb of the drawing room. Everyone inside was so happy, so at ease with one another. Would she ever find that kind of joy again? Did she have it in her?

Despite William's request, she was about to leave, to return to her room, when he caught her eye. He held her gaze, and his lips stretched into a smile just for her. Then he bestowed on her a slow wink, and it was enough to bring her back in.

"Ah, my good man, you truly have some of the best coffee I have ever tasted," Lord Merryweather said to William the next morning, leaning across the table in the breakfast room. William didn't think he had ever seen so many people in the room at once before, and he was rather shocked that all had risen early enough to partake. It had not, however, been a particularly late evening, and he knew they were all rather looking forward to the day's activities.

William tipped his own cup to the man, noting that Rosalind, surprisingly, also chose coffee instead of the usual tea most of the young ladies drank. It seemed he learned something more about the woman every day.

She gave him a small smile before Lord Harrington, at her left, re-engaged her in conversation. William found himself feeling a bit jealous of the man at having captured her attention, but quickly he told himself he was being ridiculous, for Harrington was happily married.

He was rather confused over his feelings toward Rosalind. He was attracted to her, that was for certain. She was a woman with depth of character, who had fascinating views on the world and knowledge far beyond what most women possessed. And yet, she chose to hide it from most, which he could not particularly fathom.

What she lacked, more than anything, was belief that she was worthy enough — for him, and to be on equal footing to others of the *ton*. He didn't know why she had such doubt in her own character, but he wished she would embrace who she was and all she had to offer the world.

"Good morning!" His mother swept into the room, as effervescent as usual, taking her place in the sole remaining chair, commanding everyone's attention. "I am so thrilled that today we will be having a musicale, does that not sound lovely? I know all of the young women here with us are accomplished singers or pianists, and I would so love for you all to show us your talents. We shall convene in the conservatory this afternoon!"

William snuck a quick look toward Rosalind. She had closed her eyes for a moment, as if she were trying to convince herself that this was a dream and when she opened them, his mother's announcement would go away. He felt a twinge of concern, both for her and also regarding her words from the previous evening. Perhaps she was right — perhaps she *would* be unhappy with his life. He felt his brow furrow in consternation as he sighed to himself.

When Rosalind exited the breakfast room, he followed after her and caught her hand as she entered the stairwell to return to her chamber.

"I have not yet had the opportunity to say good morning," he said with a quick smile.

"Good morning," she said in response with a forced smile of her own.

"You do not seem particularly ... pleased about the musicale."

"Not entirely," she said, nibbling on her lower lip in a way that made him want to kiss away all of her nerves and frustration.

"I have heard you sing before, at a musicale some time ago," he said. "I seem to recall you having a talent that many admired."

She shrugged. "I can carry a tune, I suppose. I am not sure anyone will want to hear it, however. The other young ladies will be more than happy to sing for you, so you should not need me—"

"Rosalind," he stopped her. "Will you please join in? For me?"

She didn't say anything, her eyes trained on his chest. Finally she raised them and looked him in the eye.

"Fine," she said, although she didn't look particularly pleased. He wondered if he was in the wrong. Should he not push her to do this? Yet he felt that she needed a bit of a prod to break down the wall she had built so firmly around herself. He wanted to help her make a crack in it, as slightly uncomfortable as it may be. Was it, however, his place to do so?

"I look forward to it," he murmured, then let her continue on her way, watching her until she rounded the corner of the stairwell and left his sight.

16

"Thank you, Lady Anne!" William's mother stood and clapped enthusiastically for the pretty young woman who, it seemed, not only played the pianoforte but accompanied it as well in a rather lovely way.

The young woman smiled prettily and nodded her head in response to the applause.

"And now we have Lady Diana," said Lady Southam, who turned to give William a knowing look as she took her seat at the side of the room. His mother had talked to him the previous evening before he retired. Not only was Lady Diana beautiful and the type of woman she knew William would appreciate, his mother had told him, but she was from a good family, her father a well-respected earl. She had but a brother, so she had a considerable dowry and would be a perfect match for William.

There was only one problem — his heart was beginning to belong to another. After all this time, all the years he thought he had waited for another woman — was it this lady instead who was to be the one for him?

Lady Diana stood beside the piano, where Lady Anne

remained to accompany her. She *was* striking, William had to admit, though his heart didn't turn when he looked at her, nor did he feel any twinge in his stomach. In fact, he felt rather uncomfortable when she turned and after looking over the assembled guests, seemed to hone in on him. He swallowed.

"Yet him I lov'd so well,
Still in my heart shall dwell;
Oh! I can ne'er forget
Robin Adair."

She had a strong, vibrant voice, one that resonated with him, and apparently the others in the room as well. She finished with a flourish, her cheeks bright and her smile wide.

"That was absolutely lovely, Lady Diana," his mother said, her applause rather embarrassingly exuberant. "And now, last but not least we have…" she looked down at the paper in front of her, apparently forgetting who else might be among their party and available to sing. "Oh yes! Lady Templeton. I was told that you have a remarkable voice and therefore should entertain us all."

All emotion masked from her face, Rosalind rose and walked over to the pianoforte, slightly unsteady on her feet, although William was sure no one else noticed. He hadn't known she played the pianoforte, but she sat down behind it, her fingers resting on the keys for a moment, as if she were summoning strength from the instrument.

Then they began to move, in a tune that he did not recognize, but one which began softly and slowly. Her voice grew with the song, a haunting, chilling melody, and the low vibrato she began with slowly began to climb, until her voice rang out through the room. How could he have forgotten a voice like hers? It seemed to pierce his very soul, and he realized it wasn't just him. She didn't have a perfect voice to be sure; he was no musician but he wasn't sure she was completely on the note or the pitch. And yet, there was something about the song, perhaps the depth of feeling that accompanied it, that meant it didn't matter if she was completely perfect.

She sang of sorrow, of a love that had not only been lost, but never found. Of the unrequited love of a woman who longed for more.

When she finished, everyone in the room was mesmerized, and when she stood from the piano, there was a pause before anyone reacted. Finally William, noting how hesitant she was looking out over them, began the applause, which everyone readily joined. It was only when Rosalind had taken her seat once more that Lady Hester leaned over and said, loudly enough for the whole to hear, "My goodness, Lady Templeton, that may have been lovely, but you've ruined the mood for the entire party!"

Rosalind said nothing, but turned to face the front as his mother congratulated them all.

William strode through the room from where he had been standing at the back, and took the seat next to Rosalind. "That was beautiful," he whispered to her, wanting so badly to take her hand and stroke the soft skin as she kept her eyes toward the front of the conservatory. "I've never heard it before. Who is the composer?"

She still didn't turn and look at him, but rather kept her gaze forward and away.

"Me."

~

WHAT HAD POSSESSED her to tell him that? Rosalind thought as she made her way down the staircase to join the party in the drawing room prior to the evening's dinner. Tonight she had decided to dispense with the gray and lavender — in fact, she hardly had a choice, given that she had worn those gowns far too many times already and the gray, while cleaned, had not quite recovered intact from its time in the pond.

She was still in purple, but tonight she wore a more vibrant shade. It was fairly simple, as all her dresses were, a striped chiffon with gold lace trim along the square bodice and hem. She had worried what some of the others would think of a recent widow in such a dress, but she finally resolved that she would let them think what they pleased. She knew she would still feel the stares, even if they were imagined, but it was time she broke free of such thoughts that really served no purpose.

Before joining them, however, she needed to speak to William. She had seen him making his way toward his office, at the opposite end of the corridor from her guest chamber. She could admit to herself that she felt something for him. She had always had a bit of a penchant for him, of course, but it went beyond that now. She was, in fact, drawn to him in a way that she couldn't exactly explain. She needed, now, to know how he felt. If he truly thought something could come of the apparent attraction they felt for one another, then she was more than willing to explore it and see what could come of it.

If not, well then, as painful as it would be, it would hurt less were she to distance herself from him now rather than in the future.

As she came closer to his office door, she heard voices from within, and she slowed her footsteps. Should she wait? Or come back? She wasn't sure if she could manage another dinner without knowing what he thought or felt.

"William, dear, I am rather displeased with you," Lady Southam's voice echoed throughout the room loudly enough that Rosalind could hear it from the hall.

"And for what reason would that now be, Mother?" William asked, with what sounded to Rosalind like a note of weariness to his tone. She couldn't hear him nearly as well as his mother, and had to inch closer to the door. She put her ear to it, feeling quite guilty as she knew it was wrong, and yet she wanted to know more of what they were speaking. What could William possibly have done that would have so vexed his mother?

"Lady Diana Watson is perfect for you — perfect! And yet, you have barely paid her any attention these past couple of days. You always told me you wanted a woman who spoke her mind, who loved social gatherings as much as you, who could command a crowd so that you did not have to ensure her enjoyment. This woman certainly is all of that and more. She is beautiful. Her parents are lovely. Her father is an earl, and she has a tremendous dowry! What more could you ask for?"

Rosalind's heart sank. Lady Southam was right. Lady Diana *was* the perfect woman for William.

"What you say is true, Mother," William responded. "However, it seems my heart has been captured by another."

"Who, then? Lady Anne? She is rather lovely, quite a vivacious little thing. Although, it may be a bit close, with Olivia married to her brother, and you still holding onto your little affection toward her but—"

"No, Mother, not Lady Anne."

"Lady Frances? She is rather dull and always wears a pointed look, I suppose you could call it, but still, she would do fine. Her parents — oh do not shake your head at me, son. I certainly hope you do not mean Lady Hester. She certainly says what she thinks, although I find she has a certain bite to her that I rather do not care for."

"Lady Templeton, Mother."

Rosalind's breath caught in her throat and she straightened, her hands coming to her cheeks. She knew William felt something for her — clearly, he had shown her that with his kisses, but to say something to his mother?

"Lady Templeton?" His mother gasped. Apparently Lady Southam was in as much disbelief as Rosalind herself. "William, whatever are you thinking?"

"Yes, Mother," he said. "I have come to know her quite well over the past few days. She is an intriguing woman. She has read more than any man I've ever known. She is intelligent, and while she does not speak her opinion often, when she does, it is worth listening to because she has clearly thought things through. She has such a depth of emotion, for both people and animals. She really is lovely, Mother."

"I thought you wanted a woman at ease in society. I can tell you she certainly is not," his mother responded. "Oh, she sits there prettily enough, but that smile is rather forced. And the song she sang today — William, it was positively ghastly. The woman must still be in mourning. You would surely not want to take such a woman on?"

"I believe I am old enough to know my mind."

"And William ... would she have any sort of dowry?"

"No, Mother."

"But ... but William, we *need* it!"

"We shall find a way without relying on a dowry."

"Will you please think about this before making any rash decision?"

"I will, Mother," he responded, before adding, "Will you leave me be, please? I have some business to attend to before coming down for dinner."

Rosalind pushed back from the door, hurrying down the hall lest she be seen when his mother emerged from the room. Skirts flying, she turned the corner, rushing down the stairs and into the inner courtyard, where she could find solitude to process all she had just heard. She pushed open the door. The greenery within was slightly overgrown due to the neglect of the lazy groundskeeper Creighton, but there was a lovely fountain in the middle, which she walked around to find her way to a stone bench in the corner. She leaned back against the solid brick of the wall, the coolness of it a balm to the heat that coursed through her body.

William wanted to pursue something with her. And yet, she was entirely all wrong for him. It didn't seem anyone felt they would make a match, not even herself, if she were to be honest. As for William—

"Lady Templeton?"

A crisp, clear voice cut through the air, and Rosalind inwardly groaned. Who could have known she was in here?

"Lady Templeton, I saw you entering the courtyard. I simply wanted to know if all was all right?"

Rosalind rose from the bench, emerging from behind the tree that had hidden her from view.

"Your Grace," she said, curtsying to the Duchess of Barre. "All is well, but I thank you for asking."

"Oh, please, we can dispense with the formalities," the Duchess waved her had in the air. "Call me Tillie."

"I — I am not sure I could. Perhaps Lady Matilda, or —"

"Do you know who I was before I married the Duke of

Barre?" the woman asked, interrupting her without apology. "I was the daughter of a shipping merchant. A prosperous one, to be sure, but a merchant, all the same. My family had no ties whatsoever to gentility, besides the fact that my very best friend, the daughter of a baron and a milliner of all things, married a duke herself. So you see, Lady Templeton — or, if I may be so bold to call you Rosalind in return — I am not much for titles and the like."

Rosalind was stunned by her speech. There had been talk, of course, of the Duchess of Barre and her humble beginnings, but she had never been quite sure of what to believe. One never knew with the gossips of the *ton*.

She finally managed a small smile for the woman who looked at her so expectantly.

"Tillie, then," she said. "Thank you for your concern."

"Now," the woman said briskly. "You must tell me what is the matter. And please do not insult me by saying once more than everything is fine. I can see by the look on your face that something has upset you, and I would be willing to bet it has everything to do with Lord Southam."

Rosalind felt her eyes widening.

"I, um, I am not sure —"

"One would have to either be blind or a fool not to see the way the two of you look at one another, and I assure you that I am neither of these things," the woman continued. "Come, let us sit and you will tell me what is bothering you. It is always much better to talk it out, you see."

Rosalind smiled at the Duchess's forwardness, and found herself being led to the very bench she had occupied but moments before. They sat, and Rosalind looked at her hands for a moment before beginning.

She told Tillie of her tendre for William, how she had simply a penchant for him until recently, when she found herself experiencing emotions toward him she hadn't thought possible. She told her of William's love for Olivia, and of Olivia's marriage to the Duke of Breckenridge. She explained her own marriage, and her arrival here at the Southam home. And then she told her of how she and William had grown closer over the past few days, and of the words she had heard his mother say to him.

Tillie was a good listener, Rosalind had to admit. She let her talk without interrupting, rather simply nodding her head with a sympathetic smile on her face.

"Well," she said when Rosalind was finally silent. "That is quite the love story, I must say."

"A *love* story?"

"Why yes! That is how you feel for our Lord Southam, is it not?"

"I am not sure ... I ... that is..."

"Well, only you can determine your true feelings," Tillie said gently, placing a hand over Rosalind's. "I cannot say my love story was simple either. The good ones never are. But what I can tell you is this. Follow your heart. Your mind may tell you one thing, people around you may tell you another. But if you stay true to yourself and what you feel, Rosalind, not what you think, then you cannot go wrong. You have one life to live. Do you not deserve to be happy?"

Rosalind didn't know how to respond. What Tillie said sounded so simple, and yet her words resonated in a way that no other advice or ideas ever had.

"Thank you, Tillie," she said, a bit of warmth radiating over her, finally. "I shall do you as you say. If Lord Southam should feel the same, then we will see what can come of it. Though whatever I feel for him, I am not sure I can find myself with a man simply as his second choice."

The young duchess tilted her head as she looked at her,

finally nodding. “That is understandable,” she said. “Though sometimes the love a young man feels is much different than that of one who has experienced some of life. You will know in your heart what is best. Simply give it time.” She took Rosalind’s hand and squeezed it before rising to her feet with an air of grace. “Now, let us have a lovely dinner, staying far from the horns of Lady Hester, shall we not?”

“We shall,” Rosalind said with a smile, finally feeling that she was no longer alone.

17

Rosalind's heart felt lifted as they walked into the drawing room, though she was slightly disappointed to find William was not yet among the guests, which was rather unusual, considering he was their host. No matter, she thought, making idle chitchat with Lady Anne and Tillie. She was grateful there were truly genuine women among the guests. It wasn't that she abhorred all social events — just those where she felt she had to make forced pleasantries.

"Can you not picture it? Oh, but she was so beautiful, and so gifted that it was hard to imagine her as anything other than Ophelia!"

Anne had recently been to the theatre in London, and was describing to them the performance of Hamlet she had recently witnessed. The girl was in love with the stage, that much was clear, thought Rosalind with a smile, knowing Anne had talent but, unfortunately, as the sister of a Duke would never, of course, find herself anywhere near a stage herself. She would have to be happy performing in the odd musicale at parties such as this one.

All of Rosalind's thoughts disappeared, however, when William walked into the room. His strides were heavy, his brow furrowed, and he already had a drink in hand, the short glass filled nearly to the rim with an amber liquid. Concern rose in her as she watched him. His fingers twitched as he looked around the room, not settling on anyone in particular.

"There you are, William!" his mother called out to him, and Rosalind could see the look of resignation on his face. "Come, darling, Lady Diana has just told us the most wondrous tale of her recent encounter with the Earl of Arrondale! She has a marvelous way of storytelling, I must say..."

Rosalind tried to block the words from her hearing. William's *mother* preferred Lady Diana, not William himself. She didn't have a chance to speak to William prior to dinner, although was pleased to find herself seated next to him.

"Lord Southam," she said, smiling at him. "How are you?" She tried to infuse in her words all of the warmth, all of the emotion she was feeling, but when he looked at her, there was a hardness to his eyes, and the slight upturn of his lips didn't reach the rest of his face.

"I am well, thank you, Lady Templeton," he said, and she was startled by the coldness of his words.

"Did you ... did you enjoy the musicale this afternoon?" she asked.

"You know I did," he said, taking a hearty swig from the glass of wine in front of him. "Did I not tell you so when I was seated next to you?"

"You did," she said, feeling a flush come over her cheeks. Why was he being so cold to her? Had he listened to his mother's words, and come to new conclusions regarding her?

"And ... the rest of your day, was it—"

"My day was fine, Rosalind," he said cutting her off. "Why are you asking such inane questions? We both know that you could care less about such trivial matters."

She sat back, feeling as though she had been slapped. What had she done to cause such a reaction from him? She wanted to challenge him on it, to ask him why he was being so ... so callous and unlike himself, but she also didn't want to draw the attention of the rest of the party. Even now, a few guests had begun to look their way. Rosalind managed a slight smile as if to show that nothing was amiss, and took a healthy swallow of her own drink before focusing on her plate.

Just an hour ago, happiness had seemed potentially within her reach. Why was it now proving so hard to attain?

WILLIAM SAVORED the burning of the liquid as he poured it down his throat before it pooled in his stomach. Sometimes, when his head ached to the extent it did now, the only way to manage the pain was to drink it away until he felt numb.

He knew he was being an ass. He would apologize later, to his mother, and, most of all, to Rosalind. He knew he was giving her the wrong impression, and he could see the hurt on her face. But at the moment, it was all he could do to make it through this dinner.

He hardly ate a morsel of food, his attention instead on his wine glass. When he finally heard his mother suggesting the ladies follow her to the drawing room, he was blessedly relieved. The gentlemen would be more forgiving if he preferred to sit in silence. He lit a cheroot and leaned back in his chair, allowing the men around him to speak as they wished. He closed his eyes as he tilted his head back, pushing his chair slightly away from the table.

William's headache had come on rather quickly after his mother had visited him in his office. He had only wanted a moment alone to see to some of his affairs, and she had come bursting in, full of opinions and ideas on what his life should be. He appreciated her concern, for it seemed she only wanted him to be happy, but why could she not trust that he was capable to find happiness for himself? He was a grown man, a viscount, and yet she felt the need to guide him on the romantic area of his life. It was rather ridiculous.

Her words about Rosalind rankled with him. True, Rosalind was not one completely at ease in many a setting. He had realized this himself. Once she felt comfortable, however, she was one of the friendliest, most direct women he knew. If only his mother could see what he saw. And if only Rosalind could see it herself. For whatever reason, she seemed convinced that she was not worthy of him, and it rankled at him that she would think so.

"I say, Southam, are you all right?"

William realized he was slightly weaving in his chair, and as he opened his eyes, he found it hard to make out the features of the men around him. He wasn't sure if it was the headache or the alcohol, but either way the world was turning hazy and he was well past the point of recovery.

"My apologies, men," he said, as he rose unsteadily to his feet. "I believe I must retire for the evening."

He began stumbling out of the room, someone — Merryweather, he thought —rising to help him. William waved him away, and instead found his valet waiting for him at the door. The man was aware of such episodes, and apparently had noticed William's sour mood earlier and knew what was to come. The man helped him to his rooms and nearly had him to the door, when he heard quick, light footsteps coming from behind him down the hallway.

"William?"

He cursed. He didn't want Rosalind to see him like this, nor did he feel like speaking to her once more when he was in such a condition.

"What is it?" He turned around, and he could see his valet looking at him with concern. "Wait for me inside, Roberts," he said. "I'll be but a minute."

He couldn't grasp the man's reply, but noted the absence of his presence, as he left him alone with Rosalind.

"I saw you leave the dining room and you seemed ... rather unwell," she finally managed. "Is everything all right?"

"I told you I was fine," he said, realizing his words were slurred and he tried to piece them together as best he could. He had to make her leave him before he said anything, did anything that he shouldn't. "Rosalind. Could you, please, leave me alone?"

She took a step back, stumbling slightly, and he reached an arm to catch her, but as he did he lost his own balance, and came toppling down over her.

Rosalind gave a bit of a shriek, and he cursed as the feeling of her soft body under his where they now sprawled on the floor felt all too good.

"William," she said, her voice coming in a bit of a pant, and he groaned, his desire for her cutting through his numbed senses. "William!" she said with more urgency this time. "I — please — you're hurting me!"

He realized then that her tiny body was absorbing the entirety of his weight, and he rolled off of her as best he could, coming to lie in a heap beside her.

"Rosalind," he said, his voice tight, as he heard the door opening and his valet come rushing out. "Leave. Me. Now."

He heard the rustle of her skirts as she rose and scurried down the hallway, her footsteps retreating. William closed his eyes in relief, finally, as Roberts put his capable hands under his shoulders and carried him into his room.

ROSALIND TOOK deep breaths as she found herself retreating once again. She wanted nothing more than to run back to her own rooms, to fling herself onto her bed, and to drown herself in her own tears.

Tillie's words, however, resonated with her, as did William's own, ironically, from a few days prior. She was better than that. She was better than this, than how William had treated her upstairs in the corridor. She had already had one husband with a penchant for drink, and that had ended rather badly. This was also the second time in a matter of a few days that she had seen William become someone entirely different than the man she thought she knew. She had forgiven and forgotten the first time, but she was becoming rather uncomfortable with the thought that this was a pattern of behavior he seemed unlikely to break.

She stepped back into the hall, taking a moment to gather her thoughts and her wits before re-entering the drawing room. It broke her heart to think that William might not be the man she had initially thought he was. She still felt drawn to him and wanted to help him with whatever he was battling. And yet ... she thought of Harold, of the man he had been and what her life with him had become. In the end, all he had wanted was to drink himself out of the reality of his current life and into another.

Rosalind wished William would share with her what was driving him to partake in the spirits as he did. For his regular demeanor was nothing like the man she had seen tonight. She realized now that his coldness upon her arrival was similar to the countenance he bore tonight. He was one man one day, and another the next. It was exhausting, the play it had on her emotions, and she didn't know how to properly deal with it.

She wanted to help him, truly she did, but she also knew that she had to put herself, and her happiness, first before she could truly love another. She wiped the tear from her eye that was threatening to release down her face, squared her shoulders, held her chin high, and returned down the stairs, crying out with a start as she rounded the corner of the landing.

"Lady Templeton."

Alfred awaited her, his big body leaning against the stairwell. He was dressed, of course, in the finery expected of him, and yet despite the cravat and well-tailored evening jacket, all she could see was the man who had stood in front of the stagecoach, who had taken her to that cottage in the woods where she had waited to die.

"What do you want?" she asked, looking around for a means to get by him.

"I take it my brother is feeling rather unwell?" He asked with a grin. "Did you find a means by which to soothe him?"

"I did nothing untoward. I was simply collecting something from my chamber," she said. "Please let me by."

"Or what?" He asked, leaning toward her. "You shall tell someone? What do you suppose will happen? You hold nothing over me, Lady Templeton, do not forget that. To ruin my reputation would be to forsake your own. And if you should forget, well, have no fear. I shall be there to remind you."

She opened her mouth to retort — though what she was to say, she wasn't sure, when movement down the corridor caught her eye.

"Lady Templeton," Hester made her way toward them. "Whatever are the two of you doing out here?"

There was a gleam to the woman's eye, but Rosalind would have none of it. The woman had attempted to ruin her friend's life by capturing her in the same sort of situation, but it would not happen to Rosalind — particularly not with Alfred.

"Nothing at all, Hester," she said, moving around Alfred and down the hall. "Is your life that dismal that you must create such entertainment and make-believe stories for yourself? It truly is rather sad."

With a smile on her face, proud of herself and her quick wit for once, Rosalind brushed past an aghast Hester and continued down the hall to rejoin the ladies.

18

He needed water — badly. William sat up in bed, running his hand over his face. His tongue felt thick in his mouth, and his head was throbbing. Not the throb of a megrim coming on, but of overindulgence. He cursed. Why could he never learn? The drink helped in the moment, but it never actually cured him of his ailment. No, it only made it worse.

He swung his legs over the side of the bed, making his way to the basin of water in the corner. He cupped his hands in it, splashing water onto his face. It helped him feel somewhat better as he leaned over the washstand, letting it take his weight as he paused for a moment.

When Roberts came in with a tray of coffee, orange juice, and pastries, William could have kissed him.

"Ah Roberts, you are a Godsend," he said to the man as he placed the tray on the bedside table. Friday followed him into the room and William reached down to give the dog a pat on the head, though Friday was much more interested in the tray of food before him. "Your timing is impeccable. How did you know this is exactly what I needed?"

The man cleared his throat as if unsure what to say, before delicately telling him, "I have been with you long enough, my lord, to know what you prefer following an evening in which you are ... feeling poorly."

William sighed and ran a hand through his hair. "I am afraid I let the drink get the better of me last night, Roberts," he said. "My head was pounding so, and I was simply doing all I could to make it through the evening as a polite host, though I apparently failed at that as well. I hope I was not rude to you, Roberts. If I was, my apologies. You know it was not my intention."

"Nothing to apologize for, my lord," Roberts said as he poured William a cup of coffee. "Although perhaps..." he paused, as if he wasn't sure he should continue.

"What is it, Roberts? Please tell me."

"Perhaps Lady Templeton may have ... received the wrong impression last night."

William groaned. "Oh, bloody hell, Roberts, what did I do?"

"I believe it was primarily your state that seemed to vex her, as it caused you to lose your footing. You were also quite adamant you wanted her to leave you be."

William closed his eyes for a moment, as images from last night came flooding back to him. He would have to apologize and explain to her what had happened.

"Very well, Roberts," he said. "Thank you for your tact. I will make amends with the lady. Now, as long as I have a cup of coffee or two before going down, I believe I shall be able to face my guests shortly. How much longer are they staying?"

"Two days, for the most of them, my lord."

"Very good," he said, though part of him wished, for once,

that the party would simply leave. "Now, Roberts, I should be dressed. I believe we have outdoor games planned for today with a hunt tomorrow. At least the weather is fine, is it not?"

As he spoke with his valet, dressed, and drank his coffee, William felt a knot of worry growing in his stomach despite his smiling face. What had he said to Rosalind, and how was he going to fix it?

BREAKFAST WAS A SOMEWHAT SHORT AFFAIR, as William had risen rather late and most of his guests had already eaten. Rosalind was finishing as William entered the breakfast room, but she kept her head down, barely acknowledging him but rather speaking with Lord Merryweather. William narrowed his eyes at the two of them, feeling the jealousy growing inside as he saw the way they smiled at one another. He pushed the food around his own plate, attempting to join in the conversation, but Rosalind was rather short and continued to pay her attentions to the other man as well as Lady Anne across from her.

He saw Lady Hester watch the two of them with something of delight beginning to grow in her eye, and eventually William gave in and engaged the woman in conversation so as to distract her.

He found no occasion to speak with Rosalind prior to the outdoor games, and now he stood in the sunshine, croquet mallet in hand, as he tried to find an opportunity to pull her aside.

She was seemingly ignoring him, however, and, finding him alone, Lady Diana continued to chatter away at him, with encouraging nods from her mother and his. His sour mood was no fault of Lady Diana's, and he did all he could to be pleasant to her.

The croquet game was taking place on the round lawn to the south of the house. The gardener had managed to somewhat clean it up for the house party, although the colorful flower border could certainly use a bit more work, William thought with a bit of a sigh as Lady Diana began speaking about some sort of outdoor costume she was wearing, although currently William could have cared less. He looked across the lawn. Today, Rosalind was wearing a pale blue morning dress that gracefully floated around her legs while she walked. Funny, he had never before been particularly interested in a lady's garments. In fact, while he cared little of what Diana was speaking about, he could not take his eyes from Rosalind.

He was pleased she had stepped out of the dull grays and muted lavenders of half-mourning. Blue looked well on her. He finally looked over to Lady Diana.

"Excuse me, my lady, but there is a matter I must attend to," he said, attempting a charming smile as he saw her face fall. It wasn't that he wanted to hurt the girl, it was simply that he did not care for her in the way she deserved, and he would prefer to maintain his distance than to pretend something was there and hurt her later on.

He made his way around the croquet wickets placed within the overgrown lawn to where Rosalind and the Duchess of Barre were engaged in conversation as they slowly walked around the group in a circle. He heard Rosalind laugh, and it warmed his heart.

"Your Grace," he said upon approaching them, offering a slight bow. "Lady Templeton. Good morning to the both of you."

"Good morning," the Duchess said with a warm smile.

William had always liked her. She was open and honest and friendly, treating all as if they were equal to her station. He supposed that was because she herself had come from a family without a title. "It is a fine day, is it not?"

"It is," he replied. "I am pleased we were able to spend it out of doors."

The Duchess smiled then looked between him and Rosalind, who was wringing her gown between her fingers. "I, ah, believe my husband may be looking for me," the Duchess said with tact. "Excuse me."

Rosalind looked down at her slippers, up at the sky, and to the side at the croquet game in the distance — everywhere but at him.

"Walk with me?" he asked, holding out his elbow. She hesitated, but finally reluctantly took his arm and nodded, and he began to lead her around the outskirts of the lawn, a copse of trees his intended destination.

"Rosalind, I must apologize for my behavior last night," he said when she remained silent, keeping her gaze straight ahead of her. "It was deplorable, and I promise I should not make it a habit."

"There is no need to apologize," she said. "Your behavior should not concern me, my lord."

"My lord? Rosalind, I said I was sorry," he said, feeling a bit heated at the way she was distancing herself from him. "I do not want you to think poorly of me, and last night I was not myself. You should know me well enough to realize that."

"William…" She stopped and looked up at him. "Are you sure we are a proper match?"

"What do you mean?" he asked, his heart beginning to beat a bit faster. "I care for you, Rosalind, you know that. I had thought you felt the same for me, do you not?"

"I — yes, I do feel for you, William, but we are such different people. You need a woman who is your equal in energy, who enjoys the lifestyle you lead, who is young, vibrant, and can offer you more than just her heart, but the financial gains that can help support your family. A woman who is like ... like Olivia. I am none of those things."

He looked around, realizing they were now hidden from view of the rest of the party. He brought his hands to her shoulders.

"Rosalind," he said, trying not to raise his voice as frustration grew inside him at her words. "I have had enough of you speaking so lowly of yourself. Where have you gotten these ideas? I do not need a dowry, if that is to what you are referring. I can bring my family back to financial prosperity on my own. You are younger than I, and you are vibrant in ways that I am only just discovering. As for Olivia — I find what I felt for her was nothing more than a young man's infatuation. My life is here for the most part, and you fit rather well within this place, do you not?"

"Perhaps what you say is true, but what of your family? William, they despise me, and I must admit to you that I am not overly fond of them."

"I understand your feelings regarding Alfred," he said, cursing his brother once again. "I promise he shall remain far from you. As for my mother, well, she talks far too much about things she does not understand, nor has any right to be involved in. Do not mind her, she'll come around. She always does. What matters most is the two of us. Tell me that my behavior has not changed your feelings toward me."

Her face wrinkled in confusion, and he brushed a strand of hair back from her forehead as he leaned in closer, wanting to bring forth the teasing, smiling side of her that he had begun to fall for.

He leaned in, his hand coming to the back of her head as he brought his lips down to hers, kissing her softly, gently, trying to tell her through the contact how much he cared for her, how much he felt for her and wanted her. She responded at first, her lips meeting the rhythm of his as they moved together, but she quickly broke contact, pushing him away and stepping back from him. His heart sank as he saw a tear run down her face while she held a hand out in front of her.

"No," she said, shaking her head fiercely back and forth. "You cannot do this, William."

"What? Kiss you?" he asked, confused, as he had thought she wanted this as badly as he.

"Kiss me, say such loving words to me, play with my emotions," she said, her eyes glossed over by a sheen of tears. "One moment you are the man you have always been, kind, humorous, and altogether lovely. Then the next moment you are cold and nasty, drinking yourself into a man that I do not even want to know yet alone be with. I have been with such a man before, William, and it did not end well for anyone involved. I have no desire to put myself through that again, to be treated in a way that only pulls from me, takes all that I have to give and rips it away."

"Your husband?" he asked, needing to know yet not wanting to acknowledge the painful existence she had likely had to endure. He thanked God that it mercifully had not lasted long for her.

She nodded shakily. "I never loved him, it's true, which may be the worst of it. But I always thought he would be a pleasant enough companion with whom to share my life. He seemed to want to marry me, particularly when I had no other offers, and he was always respectful. But then after the wedding ... he became someone else, someone I did not recognize. I knew he enjoyed the drink, as most men do, but it began to consume him. And I realized, slowly, that he drank to escape his life, to escape ... me. But I preferred it, as it meant I no longer had to endure his presence. Soon enough, we were nothing more than two souls occupying the same space, and he left my bed, thank God, the bed of a 'cold fish' as he put it, and found his enjoyment elsewhere. And I was *glad* William. Oh, I was so happy that he was no longer there. I didn't want him around, I was pleased when he was away. And then he died and I felt so ... relieved, which also made me feel like the most awful person, and I just ... I just..."

Her voice broke on a sob, and he reached out to her, offering her comfort that he wasn't sure she wanted but he would provide for her all the same, if she so chose to receive it. She hesitated but finally stepped into his arms, letting everything go, to flow from her in a release that she had clearly required for some time.

His heart broke at what she had told him. The effects of her marriage clearly still lingered. He wished he could ease her pain, take away the terrible memories her husband had left her and make things right. Unfortunately, her words regarding him were true. He knew his headaches made him into someone he was not. He wanted to explain all to her, but even to him it sounded like a flimsy, trite excuse, and he did not want to make light of her words or her feelings.

Perhaps he could take more initiative to try to overcome his ailment. He had attempted a wide variety of methods in the past, though nothing had exactly worked. He would prove to her, however, that he could change, and be the man she wanted him to be. First, though, he had to make her see how wonderful *she* truly was. As long as she loved him, all would fall into place.

"Rosalind," he said as she finally pulled back from him. He offered her his handkerchief, and she used it to wipe her face. "I have to ask you one question. Do you love me?"

Her eyes flew to his, stormy under the watery sheen overtop of them. She opened her mouth a few times as if to say something, but each time, nothing came out. Finally she looked away from him, out at the lawn, before meeting his gaze once more.

"I do not know," she whispered, and his heart fell.

"I see," he said, hearing the coldness that came into his voice but was unable to stop. "I promise I can become the man you are looking for. I promise I can change my ways. But — I need you to want me in return."

"I—" she began to speak when his mother's voice cut through the air. William had nearly forgotten they were not alone in the outdoor lawn.

"William! Where have you gotten off to? It is your turn and we are all waiting. Come — oh." She rounded the corner, stopping when she came upon them, and Rosalind took a step backward. "Lady Templeton. What is happening here?"

"Lady Templeton and I were simply having a *private* conversion, Mother," he said, giving his mother a meaningful stare. "We will take this up later, Lady Templeton. Apparently it is of utmost importance that I return for a swing of my croquet mallet."

He sauntered off to the wickets, turning to look at Rosalind over his shoulder. He sighed. Bachelorhood had been so much easier.

19

Rosalind turned over William's handkerchief in her hands. It was made of exquisite linen, his initials, W.E., embroidered into the corner. She finally looked up, willing, in vain, that Lady Southam would be gone.

"Lady Templeton," the woman said coyly, and Rosalind closed her eyes for a moment. She didn't know how much more of this she could take. She wasn't meant for playing the games of society, and she wished they would all leave her be. "What was it that you and my son were so animatedly discussing?"

"Simply the wonderful house party you are hosting, Lady Southam," Rosalind said, forcing a polite smile on her face. "Now, if you will excuse me, I am sure my own turn must be coming up soon and—"

"Before you do that," said the woman, reaching her hand out to clasp it around Rosalind's arm tightly. "We must have a word, you and I."

"I believe that is not necessary, my la—"

"Oh, but it is," she said with a wicked grin. "It seems you

have some kind of designs on my son, Lady Templeton. However, you are not the woman for him, which you know as well as I. You are lovely enough, and from a good family, but you cannot provide for William what he needs. Besides that, you are a widow without any children. How do you even know if you can even provide my son with an heir?"

Rosalind's spine stiffened as the woman spoke. She hated conflict to be sure, but not nearly as much as she despised being spoken down to by a woman such as Lady Southam. The woman's question of her fertility was far too private an affair to discuss.

"I believe William is old enough to decide for himself what he wants, Lady Southam," she said, keeping her tone polite. "And please understand, I have no designs on your son, nor anyone else. I am not one to play games. Now, if you will excuse me."

She shook her arm free of the woman's grasp and moved her feet as fast as she could without breaking into an all-out run.

"Just remember, Lady Templeton," the woman's voice rang out after her, "Marriage lasts a lifetime. Can you keep my son interested in you for that long?"

Rosalind's heart raced at her words. She tried to ignore them, not allowing the woman to see how they affected her, but they were certainly the best words Lady Southam could have chosen to convince her that a relationship between her and William might not work. Harold had tired of her after a month. How long would it take William?

No, she told herself, shaking her head. *You are better than that, Rosalind. You are smart and pretty and kind, and you deserve someone who realizes all of that and more.*

"Rosalind!" She looked up, seeing that she had nearly run into Tillie, so focused she was on her thoughts. "We wondered at where you were, and I came to find you. The game is finished, unfortunately. Lady Diana is rather adept at croquet, as it were, and soundly trounced the lot of us."

"Of course she did," said Rosalind with a bit of a sigh.

"Is everything all right?"

Rosalind shrugged, unsure of what to tell her. Everything was not all right, but what was she to do?

"Did you and Lord Southam have an ... interesting discussion?"

Rosalind sighed and told her of their conversation as best she could.

Tillie listened, nodding. When she finished, she looked off into the distance before turning back to Rosalind.

"I am no expert on matters of the heart," Tillie said, chewing her bottom lip. "But what I feel is this. First of all, do not allow Lady Southam to play with your emotions. She may believe as she chooses, but I do not think her opinion has much bearing on William. Secondly, you must learn to love yourself, Rosalind, before you can love any other. It is only when you appreciate yourself for who you truly are that you will be able to properly find love. And then you can determine if you are ready to overlook all of William's demons and love him anyway. For no one will ever truly be perfect."

Rosalind managed a small smile, realizing the truth of Tillie's words. "Thank you, Tillie," she said. "You are very wise, I must say."

"Yes," said the duchess with a laugh. "I am, am I not?"

She linked arms with Rosalind as they walked back across the lawn. "Now, I heard someone tell me of puppies here, and I would so love to see them."

"That," Rosalind said with a true grin, "I can help you with. Come." She led her toward the barn, assuming that no one would miss them for a short while. Besides, how could one be melancholy with puppies around?

"Lady Diana, you were simply marvelous today," Lady Southam trilled after all had assembled for dinner. "Wherever did you acquire such skill at croquet?"

Diana shrugged a shoulder and grinned. "I suppose it comes from having three older brothers, Lady Southam. One has to pick up such games quickly in order to remain competitive among them."

Lady Southam smiled at her before turning to William with a look of, see, is she not perfect? William refused to meet her glance, turning instead to the woman beside him, the woman who had vexed him so.

"Lady Templeton," he said as Rosalind sipped her wine. "I believe we have an unfinished conversation from this afternoon."

She raised her eyebrows, as if questioning his decision to speak of such matters in front of the rest of the party. Not that they could hear, but certainly eyes were watching them. William decided, however, that he no longer cared. He was tired of the games they played, of the way they all looked for the slightest hint of gossip they could use to provide enjoyment for themselves and topics for their everyday conversation.

Now, he simply wanted to find for himself the peace and happiness that seemed within his grasp, yet still so far away.

He had been taken aback today by Rosalind's admission that she had never felt any love for her husband, that the idiotic man had distanced himself from her. It seemed to have left Rosalind with a rather dismal outlook on love and men in general, and despite the fact that it was likely rather wrong of him, William cursed the man for what he had done to her.

He realized, however, that he was likely no better, having missed what was right in front of him for so many years. He had tried to find Rosalind this afternoon to continue their conversation, but she was clearly avoiding him. He wanted a chance to explain himself, to tell her that he could be the man she wanted, but it was proving difficult to do so. He had ensured a place beside her at dinner tonight, and while by no means private, there was no way she could escape him now.

"Rosalind," he said again urgently in her ear as she continued to ignore him. "You must speak to me."

"I said what I had to say, William," she said quietly. "I care for you, I do, but I'm not sure if I can trust any man with my heart. Can we not speak of this later?"

"Fine," he replied. "Tonight, after dinner, in the conservatory."

"All right," she said with a bit of a sigh that sent a pang to his heart. Would it be that difficult for her to speak with him? He worried at what she might say if this was how she reacted to a simple few words at the dinner table.

He turned to find his mother's stare piercing into him and he wondered at how much she had heard. For whatever reason, he knew his mother wasn't fond of Rosalind, and he didn't want her to interfere with what was happening between them.

William tried to speak with Rosalind again but found that Lord Merryweather had commanded her attention. Damn the man. He typically liked Merryweather, but in this moment he cursed his gentlemanly ways and charm. He seemed to be using it on Rosalind far too often. After dinner, he told himself. He only had to wait until then and he could have Rosalind all to himself and tell her exactly how he felt.

"ALFRED," Lady Southam hissed, as she latched onto her younger son's elbow and steered him into the empty breakfast room before he could continue past her into the drawing room to join the rest of the party.

"Mother!" Alfred said, jumping when she surprised him with her presence. "Why are you creeping around like a hunting predator?"

"I needed to speak to you before you went in with the others," she said, crossing her arms over chest. "It's about Lady Templeton."

"What about her?" Alfred asked, narrowing his eyes at her.

"She and your brother have become far too close," she said. "Your warnings toward her do not seem to be working."

Alfred sighed. His mother was getting far too fraught with worry. True, it would be a rather unfortunate turn of events were William to keep the woman around, though why he would Alfred wasn't certain. He could hardly see the fascination with her. Surely William simply meant to have his way with the widow and would then let her be on her way?

"Don't worry yourself over it, Mother," he said. "Lady Templeton will be gone soon enough once the house party is over."

"That's the thing, Alfred," she said, her grip tightening where she clung to his arm. "I think William wants more than that. I am afraid he may even want to marry the chit."

"Marry her?" Alfred scoffed. "Don't be daft."

"It is you that is being a dunce, Alfred," she said, finally letting him go and knocking a knuckle against his head. "Of all the people in London, why did you have to abduct her, a woman with no one to pay a ransom? We were looking for a payout, not for such a woman to fall into your brother's arms!"

Alfred felt anger begin simmering in his belly at his mother's words. This had all been her plan, and yes it had gone very poorly, but she could hardly blame him for it. Nor was it his fault the woman remained, a constant reminder of his failure.

"*You* told me to find a coach that was clearly from a well-to-do family with a single occupant. I did that. How was I to know that a family might have a beautiful coach but no funds to speak of?"

His mother snorted. "This is the problem with being a woman," she said. "You cannot do certain things yourself. If I could, I should now be dressed in much finer clothing with jewels in my ears."

Alfred scoffed. "Do not be greedy, Mother," he said. "Your clothing is fine enough. Besides, William would never say no to you if you asked him for more."

"While that may be true," she said with a sniff, "I can hardly tell him that I invested my allowance in your little scheme that went to nothing. You know William. He would tell me that I was being greedy and irresponsible, and would never provide me with the additional requested funds as he would know it was not for any necessities. Your brother will never understand that just because I am a mature woman does not mean that I cannot like pretty things."

"Whatever you say, Mother," said Alfred, wanting to be done with this conversation and return to the rest of their party where another glass of brandy awaited him. "May I go now?"

"Not yet," she said, with a wave of her hand. "We must be rid of Lady Templeton. She knows what we have done, and she could still tell someone and ruin all of our standing in society."

"Be rid of her?" Alfred felt his eyebrows rocket upwards. "Do you mean..."

"No, you idiot," she said with a roll of her eyes. "We are not that evil. I merely mean we must have her out of our lives, and ensure that she will not tell anyone what has happened to her. Can you imagine what it would be like for us to live here, were she married to William? She would become the lady of the house, Alfred, and you know William, he would allow her to do what she pleased and the next thing you know we would both be out and living in even more poverty than we are now. No, Alfred. You have spoken with her, and I have spoken with her, but we must now dispense with words and take action."

Alfred stared at her, understanding what she was saying but unsure what exactly she wanted him to do about it.

"What are you suggesting?"

"I am *suggesting* that you, perhaps, take up Lord Templeton on his initial counter to your ransom demand," she said. "Tell him where Lady Templeton is. He can come collect the bride that he seeks, and she will be gone from us, can marry him, and William can move on with his life and marry someone like Lady Diana, who will bring with her a fine dowry. Perhaps you can try to do better this time in your attempt to coax a bit of money out of Lord Templeton in order for him to tell you where she is, hmm?"

"Fine," he said with a sigh, reluctantly agreeing with her. "I'll do it. In the meantime, try to distance William from her, will you? You know what he's like. Once he has determined he wants something, it is hard to convince him otherwise."

"Very well," she said. "That, I shall do. In fact, I have a rather splendid idea in terms of how to do so. We may need a bit of help, but I believe Lady Hester would gladly aid us without requiring much information." She explained what she was thinking and Alfred had to grin. His mother certainly was a sly one.

"Now come," she said, as if he had been holding her back. "Our guests are waiting."

As she picked up her skirts and flounced to the door, Alfred shook his head and followed her. His mother certainly was demanding, but, he had to admit, she always seemed to get what she wanted.

20

As the party began to filter out the door to retire for the evening, William gave Rosalind a meaningful look from across the room as he exited. She responded with a bit of a nod saying that yes, she would meet him as requested, and rose to leave herself. She was nearly out the door when Alfred stopped her.

"Lady Templeton," he said with a grin that sent a chill down her spine. "You look lovely this evening."

"Thank you, Lord Alfred," she murmured, then moved to try to step around him, but he blocked her path.

"Do you have somewhere you must rush off to?" he asked, the leer remaining intact upon his face.

"Of course not," she said, trying to stamp down the heat she felt rising in her cheeks. She had never been very adept at lying. "I am simply tired and would prefer to return to my room."

"I see," he said. "Tell me, have you given any more thought to that of which we spoke?"

"And that would be?" she raised an eyebrow at him,

exasperated by William's family and the way they continued to try to push her from their lives.

"The fact that we do not want you here any longer," he said. "You have overstayed your welcome, Lady Templeton, and perhaps it is time you left us."

"We are in the middle of a house party!" she said, shocked by his forwardness. "And *you* were the one who brought me here, do you not recall?"

"Ah, yes," he said, a bit ruefully. "That was clearly a mistake."

He looked over his shoulder, at what she wasn't sure, before turning back to her.

"Well, then. Goodnight, Lady Templeton. Think on what I said."

"Good night, Alfred," she said, hearing the bite in her tone and not caring in the least. She pushed past the man, wondering how on earth he could ever be related to William, and continued on down the corridor. She reached the stairwell, but instead of going up she continued past it, then looked around the corner and slipped down the other hallway into the interior courtyard. She paused for a moment to collect her thoughts and she tried to determine what exactly she wanted to say to William.

She had never been much good at coming to a decision, especially on matters of importance. Part of her wanted nothing more than to throw herself into his arms and beg for him to love her, with both his soul and his body. The other part of her warned her away, told her it would be easier were she to reject him and his family, who seemed to want nothing to do with her anyway, and build a life for herself. Would it all not be much simpler without him and his ever-seemingly changing moods? She sighed. What to do?

She squared her shoulders and determined she would hear him out, see what he had to say, and then decide from there. If she needed time to think, she would tell him that. She had to do what was best for her, and whether that included William or not, she would determine that and follow through.

Rosalind stepped into the conservatory, stopping when she heard voices.

"And this, you see, is the casa blanca lily. It blooms but once a year, and we are ever so lucky that it has graced us with its presence during this house party."

"Oh William — do you mind if I call you William? — it is simply lovely."

Rosalind peered around the corner of the pillar near the outside entrance of the conservatory. William and Lady Diana were arm in arm as she bent low over the lily, inhaling its scent. Diana looked up at William, seeming to catch his eye, and the two shared a smile that seemed to stop Rosalind's heart. She stepped back, confused as to what this meant. Had William asked her here in order for her to see the two of them together? But why would he want to wound her so? She stepped backward, trying to escape the conservatory before they spotted her, but she tripped over a rock near the entrance of the door and stumbled, landing on her rump, half in the room and half within the courtyard. She tried to scramble to her feet, but not before she found two concerned faces peering over her.

"Rosalind!" William said with worry, bringing a hand to her back and helping her up. "Are you all right? Whatever happened?"

"Nothing..." she stammered, jumping from his touch. "Forgive me, I was just ... you see, I forgot..." she felt the pink in her cheeks. William knew very well what she was doing here, but she didn't want Lady Diana to take her for some lovesick fool, which clearly she looked to be at the moment, stalking the pair of them.

"What are you looking for?" The woman asked, and Rosalind wanted to curse her apparent helpfulness. "Perhaps I can find it for you."

"No, no, it's fine," Rosalind said quickly. "I — I actually left it in the drawing room, and so I was making my way there. Forgive me, I will use the other entrance and leave you be."

"Please stay," said William in a low tone, and Rosalind could see that he was trying to tell her something with his stare, but she didn't want to hear it any longer. She was done. Done with the games, done with his family, done with him.

"No," she said, with a slow, sad shake of her head. "I am ... tired. I believe I will quit you now. Goodnight."

She started the slow walk back to her room, tears beginning to roll down her cheeks. This wasn't meant to be, her and William. She was a fool for ever thinking that there could be something between them. She would go in the morning, she decided, house party or not. She would make her way to Olivia's house, and force herself in if necessary. Olivia would return soon enough, and hopefully by then Rosalind would have decided what to do with herself.

She made her way back to her rooms, dismissing Patty after she had loosened her dress for her. Rosalind had no wish for anyone to see her in her current state, and she preferred to be entirely alone. She had taken off her gloves and her slippers when she heard a soft knock at the door. She opened it to reveal William, who looked at her with regret on his face.

"Rosalind," he said. "I am so sorry. I was waiting for you,

and my mother brought Lady Diana and said she wanted to learn more about some of our plants in the conservatory. So I—"

"Stop," Rosalind said, holding a hand out. "It matters naught, William," she said. softly. "Your mother is right. Your brother is right. What your mind is telling you is right. We are not meant to be. I am tired of this charade, of this back and forth. I will be leaving tomorrow, William. Whatever you and I had was simply some fun in the moment when there was no one else about. Clearly we do not work in your world."

"But Rosalind, I—"

"Goodnight," she said, shutting the door in his face before he could see her dissolve into tears. She leaned back against it, hearing nothing, as if he were hesitating, unsure of what to do. Finally, she heard footsteps retreating down the hallway, and she crumpled in a ball, letting the tears fall down her face. She could feel her heart breaking in her chest, and she finally had the answer to the question he had wanted to know — she loved him.

When Patty entered her room the next morning, Rosalind asked for a tray to be sent up. She could not go down to breakfast and face them all, but decided she would instead have a cup of tea in her room before making her escape. She was sure William would allow her to borrow a carriage. Olivia's home wasn't far, and the driver could be back on the same day. She hated having to ask, but, well, so be it. It was the last thing she would ask of anyone, she vowed.

As Patty helped her fold her dresses to pack into her valise, Rosalind reminded herself to retrieve her books and her journal from where she had left them in the library. She heard a knock at the door and waved Patty away, answering it herself. Strange, she thought, as she opened it to reveal Lady Southam.

"Lady Southam, good morning," she said, taken aback at the woman coming to her bedroom. Whatever she was here for, somehow Rosalind knew it would not be good news.

"That will be all Patty, run along now. Lady Templeton, are you quite well?" The woman asked with a wide smile fixed on her face.

"Yes..." Rosalind replied, confused.

"We were rather surprised you did come down for breakfast this morning," she said, "seeing as though your betrothed has arrived!"

"My betrothed?" Rosalind said, with some shock as well as trepidation. "I am sorry, Lady Southam, but there must be a mistake, for I am betrothed to no one."

"Well, Lord Templeton has rather something of a different opinion on the matter," Lady Southam replied with a gleam in her eye. "Now, come, you must greet him."

Rosalind remained rooted to the spot, her heart racing. "I am sorry, Lady Southam, but I will not be coming down. Whatever Bart has said to you is a complete and utter lie."

"Oh, come now, my dear," Lady Southam said, all pretense fading. "How can we be sure it is the man that is lying? Or perhaps you have been playing with my son's heart when you know you are not available for anything further than a quick fling?"

"Lady Southam!" Rosalind gasped. "That is not the case at all!"

"Well, then, dear," the woman said, "You must come and explain all, for William is quite beside himself."

"Fine," Rosalind said, squaring her shoulders. She

would go and make this right. Even if she and William had no future ahead of them, he had to know that she had never lied or kept any truth from him. She stepped out into the hallway and strode down the stairs, Lady Southam following her. Rosalind could practically feel the woman's triumphant stare at her back. When she reached the bottom of the staircase and turned to the breakfast room, however, suddenly strong hands came around her and pulled her back the other way.

"Ah, Lady Templeton," said Lady Southam, turning to face her. "It seems that your unwillingness to go with Lord Templeton has put us in a bit of a precarious situation. You see, you cannot marry my son, and therefore you will be returning with Lord Templeton, no matter your feeling on the subject."

Rosalind tried to protest, but a hand from the unknown man behind her came round her mouth, and while she kicked and punched with all her might, she was no match for the man's strength. She sent daggers at Lady Southam with her eyes as she was dragged around the corner, out of the house, and deposited in a carriage, still held tightly around her arms. *No!* she cried out silently. *Not again.*

21

"You mean to tell me that you are *betrothed* to Lady Templeton?" William realized he had raised his voice but he was absolutely incredulous. There was no way that Rosalind would have promised herself to this boor of a man. This current Lord Templeton, was, in William's opinion, even worse than the first, his brother Harold. He knew Rosalind's feeling toward Bart as she had made it quite clear that she had done all she could to distance herself from him.

"I am," said the man, as he leaned back in the chair in front of William's desk and crossed one leg over the other with an air of nonchalance. He studied his fingernails as if bored with the conversation. "You see, before the death of my brother, Rosalind and I had ... well, a penchant for one another, if you will. No one knew of it, and I really shouldn't even be speaking of it now, but I'm sure all will come to light. You know how the gossips are. Anyway, now that her year of mourning is finished, it is time we were married. I thank you for allowing her to stay here during your party, but I am sure you will be relieved to know that I will now take her off your hands."

William was certainly not relieved — not by any stretch. Instead, the tension within him grew, his head pounding as his hand formed a fist, and he wanted nothing more than to knock the smug grin off Templeton's face.

Templeton's words had no truth to them, William was well aware. However, there was something else at play here that he did not want to admit to himself. Rosalind had always held back from him, had never quite given all of herself. She had issues with her husband, to be sure. And why had she run, in a carriage by herself, to see Olivia?

He put those questions to Templeton, who laughed them off with a wave of his hand.

"Come, Southam, you know how fickle women can be. She wanted time with a friend before re-entering the married life, I suppose."

"Actually, Lord Templeton," he said, "I do not find Rosalind to be a fickle woman at all, but rather one who knows her mind, her values, and beliefs and acts upon them. I have difficulty believing she would say nothing of this marriage over her entire time here."

He rose, ready to challenge the man, when his mother knocked on the door and entered before he could answer.

"Oh, William, do forgive me, I didn't realize you had company," she said with a smile on her face, inclining her head. "Lord Templeton, it is lovely to see you and we are very happy to have you here. Unfortunately, I have some news to share with you both of you."

"Yes?" William asked, impatiently, though he wondered what she could have to say that would affect Templeton.

"Well, it seems that before Rosalind knew you were here, my lord, she actually packed and left to return to you. What a silly state of affairs! If only she had better communicated with you."

"She left?" William rose out of his chair, his heart racing. Was it because of their conversation the previous night? Despite all they had said to one another and decided going forward, he could hardly believe that she would have taken her leave without a word to him. That was not like her at all. Something was afoot here, between Templeton's arrival and Rosalind's departure.

"I am sure she wanted to thank you for your hospitality but simply did not have time. You should hurry, Lord Templeton, if you would like to catch up to Lady Templeton."

"Rosalind had no horse, nor carriage," said William, feeling further perplexed as his head pounded. "How did she leave?"

"One of the grooms told me a family from town was passing through on their way to London and she decided to join them," his mother said. "It seems like a rather untoward way to travel, but Lady Templeton has always seemed somewhat ... unconventional."

Templeton let out a loud, hearty guffaw that made William cringe. "Thank you, Lady Southam. I must be my way. Good day, Lord Southam."

As Templeton made his way out the door, William felt his stomach turn over. The thought of her with another man — any man, but particularly this one — made his skin crawl, and he didn't think he could live in a world where she was in it with someone else. No. He had had enough. He would find her before Templeton did, get to the truth of the matter, and tell her how he felt.

He rose to leave when another knock sounded on the door.

"Lord Southam?" Lady Hester entered, the typical coy smile on her face as she approached him, swinging her hips from side to side. "Lady Templeton had to leave suddenly, but she asked me to give you this," she said, passing William a sealed envelope with his name written across the front.

He looked up at her in surprise. "She gave *you* this?"

"She was in a rush," the woman said simply, then turned with one last look over her shoulder.

He ignored her, and instead found his opener, broke the seal, and took out the folded paper.

Dearest William, it read.

I must apologize for telling you this through a note, but I could not bear to say this to your face. I appreciated our time together, and you know how I have come to care for you. My feelings for you, however, are those of a friend. I realize now that we do not belong together, and I am sorry if I made you believe otherwise.

Please, do not protest or come after me. I have chosen a life with Bartholomew. It will be not so different from my life with Harold. We may not be in love, but can live together peacefully.

I hope you find happiness with a woman such as Lady Diana.

Until we meet again,

Rosalind

William sat back heavily in his chair, stunned as the letter fell from his fingertips to the desktop. He had thought what was between them was so much more than what she had written. Perhaps, however, he was being a fool. They had known each other since they were children, but they had only truly come to be aware of one another over these past couple of weeks. Was that enough time for any sort of true feeling to develop? And yet ... when he thought of her, the emotion that coursed through him was unlike anything he had ever felt before. He had imagined himself in love with Olivia for so many years, but when he thought of her now, he knew it had been nothing but a young man's infatuation with a striking woman. Rosalind might not be as forward, as confident, nor as vivacious as someone like Olivia, or even Diana, but she had a joy of life that she shared with those that were closest to her, with those she felt mattered enough to draw in.

She may not enjoy a crowd, but the conversations she had were of a genuine nature so rarely found. Her heart was true, and she put so much ahead of herself. She would lose a night of sleep to care for new pups, she would treat any and all as her equal, and she would stop at nothing when her values were questioned or when she had to fight for those she loved.

Rosalind was so much more than what others saw when they looked at her, and he — he *loved* her. He fell back in his chair as the revelation hit him like a punch in the gut. He really, truly loved her. He was astonished. He had never thought it was possible to have this depth of feeling for someone. And yet apparently she wanted nothing to do with him. She would prefer the life she had known, with a man so similar to the one she had left.

William stepped into the hall. He had to know that she had left of her own accord, had to be sure it was true that she didn't want him. "Patty!" he called, seeing the maid scuttling around the corner. "Were you with Lady Templeton today?"

"I was, my lord," she said with a dip of her head.

"Is it true she chose to leave?"

"Y-yes my lord," she said, clearly seeing the ferociousness of his glare. "We packed her bags this morning, the two of us together."

It was sure then. Like Olivia before her, he was nothing more than a friend.

He dismissed her, returning to his office, walking over the sideboard and pouring himself a large snifter of brandy. He drank the whole thing down before pouring himself a second, despite the fact it was only halfway through the day. He knew he had a house of guests, but currently, he didn't really care, as he thought only of his pounding head and broken heart.

She didn't like him drunk, he thought, taking another sip. *Well, I am sorry Rosalind*, he thought. *But you lost any right to an opinion when you left me.* And now, he would do whatever he damn well pleased.

WHEN ROSALIND HAD WOKEN that morning, she knew it would not be a particularly pleasant day. However, she could never have realized just how terrible it would be.

She fought Alfred all the way back to the wretched cottage in the woods. Despite being unable to see his face, she had soon realized it was he who held her. Who else would conspire with Lady Southam? Of course he would bring her back here. The man didn't seem to have any creativity within his soul.

When she had been here before, she had been distraught, panicked, for she had no idea where she was or who held her. Now, it was different. She knew who he was, what he was doing, *why* he was doing it, and all she felt was an anger that simmered from deep within her soul.

As he led her through the woods, she stepped on his toes, elbowed him in the stomach, tried to knee him in the groin, but he managed to evade her, being far larger and stronger. It was times like these she wished she had more strength and resilience.

By the time they reached the cabin, she had exhausted herself, and it was all she could do to stay on her feet as he pushed her through the door.

"You will not have to stay for long this time," he said in a nonchalant tone. "Just until your betrothed comes to collect you."

Bart, she thought, realizing she would far prefer Alfred as a captor than Bart, she thought as Alfred closed the door behind him, and she heard the scrape of wood as he locked it. Alfred was greedy and foolish, but she had come to realize he would not actually hurt her — for if he had wanted to, he could have killed her the first time he had abducted her once he realized she was worthless. He had not, however. Instead, he had asked his brother for help.

Now she thought of William, wondering what he would do at her disappearance. Would he search for her? Or had her rejection of him been so severe that he would be happy to be rid of her?

She kicked at the rotting floorboards, making her way gingerly over to the rough-hewn table and stools in the middle of the small room. There was what passed for a cot in the corner, but she had inspected it last time and realized there was no way she could even sit upon it. Rosalind knew that there was no alternate exit besides the door, and nothing within that would allow her to fashion an escape for herself.

Although ... Alfred had spent some time here when William had banished him from the house. Was there any chance he had left something behind? She began her search, determined to find a way to escape. This time, she refused to be the victim.

22

William likely would have drunk himself into a stupor had Merryweather not come to find him.

"Southam!" the man said from the door. "We were wondering what had kept you. Some of the men are eager to get to the hunt if it is still planned for today?"

"Ah yes," he said, rising a bit unsteadily to his feet. "The hunt. Apologies, Merryweather. Yes, I will have the staff ready everything for our departure and will be but a moment myself."

William sighed as Merryweather nodded and left. He brought his fingers to his temples, closing his eyes. He had entirely forgotten about the hunt, but of course that was what many of the men had come for and he couldn't very well suggest another lead it.

He forced his legs to stand and dragged himself into the hallway. As he turned to ascend the stairs to his chamber, he was surprised when the Duchess of Barre and Lady Anne stopped him in the corridor.

"Lord Southam," said the Duchess, assuming an air of

regality that was rather uncommon of her. "Your mother has informed us that Lady Templeton has departed to return to her *betrothed*?"

"So it would seem," he muttered, though he hadn't finished the sentence before the two beautifully styled heads in front of him began shaking to and fro.

"That cannot be," cried Lady Anne. "Rosalind is certainly not betrothed to anyone, especially the horrific Lord Templeton. Why, he's even more of a rotter than her first husband."

"That, I can agree with," he said with a sigh. "But she has left a note, and it seems that she has, truly, decided to leave and go to him."

The Duchess waved her hands in the air, disregarding his words. His head was somewhat fuzzy from the drink, and he wished she would stop moving so quickly.

"Are you certain she wrote it herself? Let me see it," she said, to which he shook his head. She might be a duchess, but he certainly was not going to share with her private correspondence regarding his unreturned feelings toward Rosalind. He would not make himself a laughingstock.

"I am sorry, Your Grace, but I cannot do that," he said. "I can tell you that she was very clear that she has deliberately chosen her current path."

"But she hates Lord Templeton," the Duchess said, surprising William. "She came here to escape him, Lord Southam, and you must realize that if there is any man she longs for, it is you."

He refused to allow her words to provide him any sense of hope but instead resolved to remain resolute.

"You are quite mistaken," he said. "Now, excuse me, but I must prepare myself to leave for the hunt."

He placed a foot on the stairs, but couldn't take his mind

from what the Duchess had said. Was there any chance that Rosalind had not written the letter? He doubted it, yet ... the only time he had ever seen her write before was in that notebook of hers. He tried to recall her penmanship, but couldn't bring it to his mind. An unbidden image of the journal amongst her belongings in the library came to mind. But no, if she had left, she surely would have taken it with her. It was one of her most valuable possessions.

As much as he told himself he was being foolish, he found his feet taking him down the corridor toward the library. He pushed open the door, finding one or two men amongst his collections, and made his way over to the corner — her corner, by his way of thinking now. He picked up the stack of books tucked in the small corner cabinet and rifled through them. Ah, so she had decided to read *Waverly*, he thought, a small unbidden smile coming to his lips that she'd trusted his recommendation.

He halted as he came to one book that stood out among the others, a green leather-bound volume only half filled with notes, the rest empty, awaiting her thoughts.

These were her notes. And yet, would she really leave them behind? He thought that rather odd, and a sense of unease began to replace his melancholy, sobering him up and focusing him. His eyes skimmed over a passage, one in which a young woman yearned for a gentleman who she had always known but who had never seen her in return.

Why, she is writing a novel, he thought with a start, her words intriguing him, making him want to read more. Before he could do so, however, he quickly observed that this writing did not match to the note. It was similar, to be sure, but — the Duchess of Barre had been right. Rosalind had not written that note, he realized, his heart beating fast.

Hester had lied to him. Who had given her the note, and where was Rosalind?

"Ah, my dear Rosalind," Bart kicked the door shut as he strode into the room. "How lovely you are here waiting for me."

"Bart," she said, hearing the anger in her own voice as the man she hated with such passion walked toward her. "What is this meaning of all of this?"

"Is this any way to greet your soon-to-be husband?" he asked, with a leer on his face as he advanced toward her. "Especially when I have come all this way to collect you?"

"You have wasted your time," she said, trying not to let her voice tremble, despite the mad beating of her heart in her chest. Now was the time to show him the strength that had always been within her. "I will *never* marry you."

He shrugged, clearly not affected by her words. "You have not much choice anymore, my dear. This will all be much simpler if you do not fight it."

"Why me, anyway?" she asked, throwing up her hands in exasperation. "There are plenty of eligible young women looking to be married. I hate you. I'm sure your brother told you that I am not worth marrying. So why?"

Bart sighed as if it was a chore to speak of this with her, but he continued. "Surely you have heard of my reputation."

She had heard whispers, although no one had ever fully explained the reason why fathers were reluctant to wed their daughters to such a man. Bart was a second son, true, and not a particularly attractive one at that, with a paunch belly and facial features that were always pulled into a sneer of some sort. She had figured those were reasons enough but apparently there was more.

She shrugged, needing to know as much as she didn't really want to. "I do not pay attention to the gossips."

"Well, as you will soon learn," he said, so close to her now she could smell the lingering ash, fish, and whatever else he had for lunch on his breath. She tried not to recoil in her disgust. "I have certain sexual tastes that many young women are not fond of feeding. Unfortunately, I had an encounter with a particular woman of the *ton* some years ago, and she found it her duty to share with others what they could expect from a dalliance with me. Alas," he sighed, "I have not had much opportunity to find a woman who would share such proclivities, besides those who are paid for. Hence, I have not found a wife to this point in time. It didn't much concern me until now. For now, I am an earl, and I need heirs."

He leaned in, his face a breath away from hers. "And you are going to give them to me."

Rosalind was horrified. If the *ton* knew of this, her father must as well. And yet, he would allow her to be married to such man? Did he care nothing of her at all?

"Get away from me," she ground out, pushing back against his chest. He hardly moved at all, her small, slight build being no match for his round, heavy one.

"I think not," he said, laughing. "I shall do as I please."

Rosalind closed her eyes for a moment. What was wrong with her? Why had she not taken her chance for happiness with William? If she had, she would not find herself in such a predicament. She had been stupid, too lost in her own self-doubt. She had let her parents, their questioning and needling from the past invade her future, and in doing so had prevented her own happiness.

Not anymore, she resolved. She would fight for what she wanted, for the future that was still within her grasp. But first she had to get away from Bart.

She lifted her hand ever so slowly so as not to attract his attention, up his chest until it neared his throat.

"Bart," she said, her tone even, determined to show no emotion on her face. "I said, *get away*."

He looked down now, and jumped back hurriedly when he saw the blade in her hand at his neck.

"What do you think you are doing with that?" he asked, his mouth agape, and it was now her turn to smile, despite the fact that she was still near trembling with fear and anticipation.

"Your *friend* Alfred used that wretched cottage for a few days and seemed to have forgotten to clean up after himself," she said. "He left a few utensils in the cabinet, including, luckily, a hunting knife."

"You would never have the nerve to use it," he said, his initial surprise having fled, to be replaced by his usual smugness. "You are timid, Rosalind. You are not strong enough, you are not sure enough, you are not confident enough to do anything more than make idle threats. Be the good girl you always are, put the knife down, and come home with me."

"I will not," she said, though in her heart his words pulled at her. He had a point. She wasn't sure if she was capable to do anything with the knife besides point it at him.

"Rosalind," he said again, taking another step toward her. "Even if you do escape from me, what are you going to do? I've heard you have a penchant for Southam, but you must know the man cares nothing for you. His brother said you have been mooning around here for days, trying to get him to notice you, but Southam is to marry the beautiful Huntington girl. Do not make a fool of yourself, Rosalind. You have nowhere else to go but home with me."

Rosalind shook her head, trying to clear it. She felt, in her heart, that William had feelings toward her, but were they enough? She knew his family, and likely his own mind, was telling him that he should be with a woman like Diana. Hell, Rosalind herself had told him to be with Diana. And yet, despite her head telling her how wrong she and William were for each other, despite the struggles they would have or the adversity they would face, her heart told her that there was no other for her. She loved him, and would find no joy in life without him. After everything she had been through, did she not at least owe herself the chance to see if she could be happy?

"You're wrong," she said, now resolute. "And I do not appreciate you trying to get into my head. Now, Bart, do not come any closer."

The only warning he gave her was the wicked smile before he shot his hand out to try to wrest the knife from her. As he did so, she lashed out with her arm to push him away, but instead felt her entire body jar as the knife hit something solid. As he screamed, she realized she had sliced the knife into his shoulder, where it now jutted out. As he grabbed the hilt, she overcame her shock and scampered around him as fast as she was able, reaching the door and running up the hill with all the speed she could muster, toward safety — toward William.

23

William patted his horse's neck as they approached the stables. He had looked throughout the house for Rosalind, had questioned all of the servants and found nothing. He had excused himself from the hunt, spending his time searching the yard and the house for her. He questioned the men before they left for the hunt, but none said a word. Even Alfred and Richard seemed in the dark.

The exertion and fresh air helped him emerge from the shadows that engulfed him and the pain that radiated through his skull. And yet, as good as it felt, his thoughts never wavered from a pretty girl with chocolate brown hair and eyes that haunted his soul. He thought on all she had said to him, on what the Duchess of Barre and Lady Anne had told him, and of her own words, written on the pages of her novel. Could it be? Did she really love him, as he did her? But what did it matter, if he couldn't find her?

He sighed from the door of the stable as he looked at the group returning to the house. He knew Rosalind wouldn't have returned to the home of Lord Templeton. So where had she gone? He gave his horse one final pat, looking over at the dogs. They were a few days old now, and were snuggled up next to their mother. They reminded him of Rosalind, he realized, and emerged in the late afternoon sunshine to find Friday sprinting up the hill toward him.

"Hey there, boy," he said, bending to greet the dog. Friday had other ideas, however, bounding around William, barking relentlessly before running back down the hill while William stared after him, perplexed by his behavior. Friday returned, barking and running down the hill and back up again toward William, who finally realized the dog wanted him to follow him.

"I'm a bit busy, boy," he said, but the dog was relentless.

"All right, then," he said. "You are quite persistent. I'm coming."

He followed Friday, who set a fairly good pace. William felt slightly ridiculous following the dog through the brush and into his woodland. For all he knew, the dog wanted to show him a bird or a rabbit he had managed to snare.

Finally, Friday stopped, sniffing around the base of a huge fir tree that had been on the property for years. His bark changed to one of excitement, and William thought he heard a "shh" coming from the other side of the fir.

"Hello?" he called out. "Is someone there?"

"Oh, William!" a voice cried, and he started in surprise and relief as Rosalind emerged from behind the tree. She looked rather bedraggled. Her hair was trailing down her back and around her shoulders, free of its pins, the long straight brown locks rather askew. Her cheeks were flushed, as if she had run a great distance, and the soft yellow of her dress was torn and muddy, clearly from a romp through the woods.

"Rosalind!" he exclaimed as he made his way hurriedly

through the brush toward her, taking her in his arms and grasping her tightly to him. She finally let out a bit of a strangled noise, and he realized just how tightly he was holding her, so overcome he was with relief. He let her go but stayed close to her. "Whatever are you doing out here?"

"We have to go," she said urgently, as Friday jumped up on her in excitement that he had managed to reunite the two. "Bart he's — he's after me. I tried to run toward you, to find the house, but I became utterly lost. I have no idea where I am or how to get back, and finally Friday somehow happened upon me, quite by accident, I'm sure, and I tried to follow him, but he was too fast for me. Then I heard Bart's voice calling out for me, and I hid. We must go now, before he finds us."

"Let him," William said, his voice resolute. "But why — Rosalind, what happened?"

"Your brother and your mother," she said, and he was surprised at the vehemence in her tone. "They truly do not want us together, William. So much so that they made some kind of an arrangement with Bart. Your mother lured me out of my room, your brother dragged me back to this cabin, and there I was left to wait for Bart, who was going to take me back to his home."

William's eyes widened at her words. What she was saying could not possibly be true — could it? Could his mother and brother be so evil as to work against his happiness, for all he ever wanted? And for what? He thought about it for a moment as he searched her face, which was open, earnest, willing him to believe her, to understand her. And the truth of the matter was that he did. As much as he wanted to deny it, he knew how underhanded his family could be. And yet, he could hardly believe they would go this far.

He gently reached out and ran his hands down her bare arms.

"Are you hurt?" he asked, bringing his thumb to her chin and looking her over.

"Nothing but a few scrapes from some offending branches," she said with a bit of a smile.

"Good," he said, and feeling so very grateful to have her here, safely with him, that he reached out and pulled her to him again but more gently this time, holding her close with his arms wrapped around her. He breathed her in, smelled the rose of her hair, felt her warmth through the muslin gown, and he realized deep within his soul that he never wanted to let go.

"Rosalind," he said softly, finally releasing her with a kiss upon the top of her head. "I—"

"Well now, I am sorry to interrupt this tender moment, but I will be collecting my bride now, Southam."

William turned at the words, his eyes narrowing as Lord Templeton approached. The man clearly was not one used to such exertions as trampling through the brush chasing after young women who did not want to be found, and he looked rather disheveled himself, though more than anything, he looked angry — very angry.

Friday crouched low in front of them and growled at Templeton, while William pulled Rosalind behind him as he faced Templeton. It was only then he noticed the blood coating his left arm.

"Templeton," he said, as authoritatively as he could. "What you have done here is despicable. Return to the house, gather your carriage, and be gone."

"I think not," the man said with a sneer, though it was obvious he was beginning to weaken somewhat. "I am not leaving without my little bitch of a wife."

"I am not your wife," came Rosalind's voice from behind him, as much as William tried to quiet her. "Nor will I ever be."

"Do you truly think so?" he asked, and with great relish he pulled a firearm from behind his back, causing Rosalind to gasp. "I believe I hold the power now."

"Templeton," William said, holding up his hands in a sign of surrender as he slowly walked toward the man, hoping Templeton would move his aim from Rosalind to him. "What is your plan here? Do you truly believe you can take Rosalind against her will, spirit her away in your carriage, and force her to marry you without consequence? Come, man. We are past the point. This no longer has any sort of ending for you besides one of punishment. However, you still have a way to lessen it. Simply leave — by yourself, of your own free will — and never come back. Forget Rosalind, forget me, and return to your home, where you can happily live out the rest of your days."

"You don't understand," Templeton said, his glare darkening. "My brother had everything. He was the focus of my father for our entire lives. He became the earl, was provided with a wife, and all the riches he could want. And he cared not for any of them. I now want all that he had. You see, once I want something, Southam, I am determined to get it. Harold is out of my way now, so both the earldom and his bride can be mine. After all I have been through, I will not allow the likes of you to get in my way."

William heard Rosalind gasp and he looked over to her, seeing her mouth agape as she stared at Templeton.

"You killed him," she said in almost a whisper. "You pushed your own brother down the stairs — how could you?"

"Oh come, Rosalind, it's not as though you even liked the

man that much," said Templeton with bluster. "If anything, I did us all a favor to be rid of the boor."

"You believe yourself to be any better?" William asked with a growl. "I should hardly think you to be a fair replacement. And do you not suppose the lady has a right to choose for herself?"

"Do you truly think you have any justification to be so self-righteous?" Templeton ground out, as the men came close to one another. "You, whose own family has conspired against her, not once, but twice? What do you think would ever come from a union between the two of you? Are you going to banish your own mother and brother in favor of a woman?"

William paused for a moment, then turned and looked at Rosalind, holding the gaze of the green eyes that stared back up at him.

"For the right woman — of course."

They were both silent for a moment as she closed the distance between them, taking his hand as they stared at one another, seemingly forgetting, for this brief moment in time, Templeton and all of the trials that awaited them.

"Enough of this," Templeton said, cutting through the thick tension that hung in the air. "Time to go. Rosalind, you're coming with me. Southam, home to your party. And call off your dog, or I will shoot him."

"Friday, down," William said, but stood tall in front of Templeton, who was shorter but much stockier. William knew he would likely have a fair bit of strength on the man should it come to it, though Templeton held the gun in hand. William leaned down and whispered in Rosalind's ear. "When I move, run to your left — quickly." As Templeton raised the gun to William's face, William charged at him, catching him round the middle. Templeton gave a grunt of surprise as the breath shot out of him and he went flying backward. William threw a punch, and the two scrapped on the ground. William grunted as a tree branch bit into his back, before he flipped himself and Templeton over. He was holding the man down when suddenly the world went black before him as Templeton whacked the gun against his temple with a crack.

William fell backward, his vision hazy. He tried to push himself up to a sitting position, but felt nearly no ability to raise his body. Templeton leaned over him, holding the gun in front of him with a smile on his lips underneath a nose that William had bloodied, and all William could do was pray that Rosalind had run fast and far, so that at the very least she could escape this man and the future he would hold for her. *Be smart, Rosalind,* he willed. *Follow your heart and find the love you deserve.*

He closed his eyes and braced himself for the impending shot, but it never came. Instead he heard a muffled groan and the sound of something heavy hitting the forest floor. His eyes flew open to the most beautiful sight he had ever laid eyes on — Rosalind, hair floating around her face in a halo as the rays of sunlight that peeked through the forest canopy of leaves engulfed her.

William pushed himself up to a seated position, holding a hand to his head as he looked around him.

"Rosalind?" He stared up at her, and she wore a slight smile on her lips. "What did you...?"

"He was going to kill you," she said simply, dropping the rather large, broken tree limb from her fingers, as if suddenly it had become to heavy to hold onto anymore. "I did what I had to."

He shook his head in amazement, then reached his arms up toward her and she came to him quickly, lying nearly on top of him as he held her as close as possible, breathing in the scent of her hair, so fresh and clean, like the woodland he laid in.

William opened his eyes when he heard a bit of a grunt beside him. He turned his head to see Templeton twitch, though Friday stood overtop of him, pinning him to the ground.

"You hit him hard, love, but I'm not sure it was quite hard enough," he said. "We best go before he wakes up."

"What are we to do about him?" she asked, leaning back and looking into his face, brushing her fingers lightly over the bump he could feel beginning to form on his head where the bastard had hit him.

"Not to worry," he said. "I have a plan."

24

Rosalind had known she was near the house, but simply hadn't been able to find her way. Now with William guiding her with his words, his arm slung over her shoulder as he stumbled beside her, she felt a bit of a fool as she realized just how close the house was.

"Not your fault, love," he said, smiling at her. "These woods can be a bit confusing. You simply needed your guide."

"Apparently I did," she said with a rueful grin. "Although you are a much heavier guide than I would have imagined."

He chuckled and seemed to try to shift some of his weight off her. He had attempted to make his way back to the house unassisted, but kept wavering off the path. When Rosalind had offered to help, he had resisted at first, but eventually relented and they had been slowly making their way forward since. Friday had long since returned to the house, apparently feeling his work as protector had been completed.

Rosalind looked over at him. "It's all right," she said. "You can give me more of your weight."

His face tightened in apparent pain and he shook his head. "I'm fine."

"No, you are not," she insisted. "I'm stronger than you think."

"Now that," he said, raising a finger in the air as if to emphasize his point, "Is entirely true, and I am pleased that you have come to realize it."

She blushed, understanding his words went beyond the physical efforts she was making.

As she looked at him closely, she could tell he was trying to hide his discomfort. He gave a slight groan as he brought a hand to his head.

"What is it?" she asked, concerned.

"It — it seems the blow to my head has triggered the return of one of my headaches."

"Your headaches?"

"Yes," he said with a sigh as he nodded. "At times, particularly when I feel under any sort of pressure, my head starts to pound furiously. I can hardly describe it, but the ache within overcomes all else and it is all I can do to even function. That is why I overindulge, because I am trying to rid myself of the pain."

"Oh, William," she said, her eyes wide as she thought back now to his sudden mood swings, the way his hand always came to his head in what she thought was a simple habit. "Why did you not tell me?"

"It seems rather foolish and a poor excuse for my untoward behavior," he said with a shrug. "And it will not go away. I have tried everything, seen every doctor, and short of boring holes in my head — which some wanted to do — nothing seems to work. Although, I must say, as strange as it sounds, your presence brings about a calm that seems to help dull the pain in the early stages."

He paused for a moment, the silence stretching between them as she thought on his revelation. "I suppose I should have told you sooner," he continued. "I was a bit ashamed, to be honest. I did not want you to know how routine it had become, that what you have witnessed were not solitary incidents, but rather a villain that will not be vanquished. I do not know if it will ever go away, Rosalind. It's something that I shall always have to deal with, that will continue to make me into a bit of a beast, I'm afraid."

"Yes, you should have told me, you silly, stubborn man," she said, shaking her head as she pointed a finger into his chest. "Oh William, I kept thinking you were pushing me away, that you wanted nothing serious with me, when all this time it was something else that was bothering you? If nothing else, I could have helped you!"

"There is no help for me," he sighed. "I told you, I have tried it all."

"When I was young," she said, slowly, her heart warming as she remembered, "I had a nursemaid. Her name was Gretchen, and she was ever so wonderful. She showed me love when there was none to be had in my house, when my parents were busy with society, and I had no one else to keep me company. Anyway, she suffered much the same. Whenever her headaches appeared, she concocted an herbal remedy. I remember the ingredients, peppermint being the strongest. She would extract it from the leaves, rubbing the scent over her temples, her neck, and drinking a tea of it. It never entirely did away with the ache, she said, but it certainly dulled the pain some. Have you ever attempted something like that?"

"No," he said with a shake of his head. "Though I suppose it's worth a try."

"Wonderful," she said, happy he had agreed. "We shall

try it then. You must understand, William, whatever might help or not, you do not have to keep anything from me. I will be there to help you."

He gave a quick nod before stilling his head, apparently the movement being too much, though he managed a smile. "Understood, my lady."

When they reached the house, he suggested they enter through the servant's doors to avoid the attention of the guests or his family. She quickly agreed, and despite the horrified looks they received from the servants, they assured them all was well. William asked them to say nothing and they agreed, their loyalty clearly with their viscount and not his mother. Rosalind could understand why. Lady Southam had certainly not made herself particularly beloved by the servants of the manor.

William interlaced his fingers with hers, and Rosalind felt warmth shoot through her, running up her arms and through her body with a tingle. It felt so right, so lovely to be with him, despite the fact that there was still so much unspoken, and many an obstacle between them and the life she tried not to allow herself to hope for. She had always dreamed of loving with all of her heart, of what it would feel like to be completely loved and accepted in return. She had not, however, allowed herself to consider the possibility of it coming true for fear of how much it would hurt for it all to be taken away from her.

And yet, despite how hard she had tried to resist, how much she had pushed William and all she felt for him far away from her, she realized she had completely lost her heart to him. She could only hope that he would feel something of the same in return, that they could find a way forward together.

Now, however, was not the time to tell him of this. Not

when Bart would be appearing from the woodlands where she had bashed him over the head with a fallen tree branch. She could hardly believe what she had done. If she had taken even a moment to contemplate her actions, she knew she could never have gone through with it, but when she had seen him holding the gun up to William, she had acted on instinct. She had hardly been able to lift the branch, but she found just enough strength to bring it down over his head. It had been a rush that she couldn't describe, that she wasn't sure she could duplicate if she had to again, though if she ever had to do anything to save William's life, she knew she would do all she could.

"Rosalind," he said softly as they reached the entrance to the hallway. "Slip up to your room and change. Do not let anyone see you. Stay there until I come for you, all right?"

She nodded and he eased the door open a crack. Apparently seeing no one in the hall, he gave her a quick nod and put a hand to her hip as she slipped through the door and up the stairwell. She stole a quick look back at him as he watched her go. He gave her a wink before she slipped up the stairwell as fast as she could.

Rosalind entered her room, collapsing against the bed as the adrenaline began to drain out of her and she considered all that had just occurred. She jumped when she heard a soft knock at the door, freezing as she tried to remain silent.

"It's me, my lady — Patty," came the soft voice, and Rosalind cautiously made her way to the door. "Lord Southam asked that I come help you," she said, so quietly that Rosalind nearly didn't hear her. She opened the door and the maid slipped in, looking over her with wide eyes.

"I must apologize, my lady," she said, her eyes downcast. "I told the lord you had left."

"You could not have known," Rosalind assured her. "All is well now."

"Oh, my lady, you look a fright!" she said, then clapped a hand over her mouth as she realized what she had said. "That is — I mean —"

Rosalind gave a soft laugh. "Not to worry, Patty, I know how I must look. Thank you for helping me."

"Of course," the girl said with a nod before reaching behind her to help her out of her dress. "Unfortunately we canno' bring you a bath without attracting much attention, but we'll wash you up as best we can."

"Thank you Patty, I appreciate it," said Rosalind with a smile as the girl helped her wash and change.

"If that will be all, my lady?" Patty asked and turned to go.

"One other thing," Rosalind said, holding up a finger. "Can you have Cook prepare something for Lord Southam?"

She proceeded to outline what she could remember from her nursemaid's concoction, and while the girl looked slightly puzzled, she agreed with a nod and slipped out of the room.

Now, thought Rosalind, she just had to wait.

After speaking with Roberts and his steward, directing them as to where to find Templeton, William cleaned himself up best he could and took a long drink of brandy before joining his guests in the drawing room. After the hunt, many of the men had deeply entrenched themselves in card games while the women were in the drawing room or the conservatory as they did whatever it was women did to while away the time. William would have liked more time to himself to try to recover from his pounding head, but he couldn't afford to miss his window of opportunity.

He found the person he was looking for in the conservatory, and he breathed a sigh of relief that his plan would hopefully fall into place. It was a bit wicked, he had to admit, but it was nothing short of what was deserved and would ensure the happiness of the person he loved more than any.

"Lady Diana," he said, greeting the woman where she sat with her mother in the drawing room. "May I speak with you a moment?"

"Of course," she said with a smile, and rose to follow him. He walked her out of the room to the conservatory, strategically positioning them on one side of a large statue.

"Lady Diana," he began. He felt slightly boorish for having this conversation with her to so conveniently suit his agenda, but at the same time he would have to speak with her either way. Everything he said to her would be the truth. "Over this past weekend, it has not been lost on me that many, including our own mothers, would like to see us matched with one another."

"I would agree that would be the case, Lord Southam," she said with a bit of a laugh. "Your mother in particular."

"Yes," he said ruefully. "She is not particularly tactful. I should have spoken to you of this some time ago. The truth is, Lady Diana, that while you are a delightful young woman who I do enjoy spending time with, my heart has been otherwise engaged. I am not sure if the lady will have me, but I must do what I can to make it work with her."

She nodded, a knowing smile on her lips. "I understand, Lord Southam, and I cannot say that I have been completely oblivious to your affections. I have enjoyed my time here, however, and have found all to be quite pleasant company."

"I am glad to hear so," he said. "I value your friendship and appreciate your presence."

"I do appreciate your straightforwardness," she said with a smile. "Most men would not be so truthful, and I must say it is refreshing."

"Thank you," he said, feeling relief flood through him that she would hold no ill will toward him. "I wish you the best in your pursuit of happiness."

"And I you, Lord Southam," she said. "Oh, and best of luck with your mother. I feel you will need it."

He laughed at that. "I feel you are right."

As she walked away, William didn't let himself become too satisfied with himself. The first part of his plan had worked. But there were pieces that had yet to fall into place.

25

William did a bit of a turn about the conservatory, and as he returned to the location of his original discussion, he pretended to be shocked when he came upon Lady Hester and Lady Frances on the other side of the statue.

"Oh, Lady Hester!" he said, hoping he was able to properly conjure surprise on his face. "You are just the person I was looking for."

"Me, my lord? Oh, how lovely," she said with a bit of a catlike smile and a knowing look at Lady Frances.

"Might I have a moment?" he asked, inclining his head toward her.

"Of course," she said as Lady Frances rose and gracefully walked away.

"Lady Hester, I know we have not had ample opportunity to come to know one another well," he began, and she smiled, placing a hand on his arm.

"Do not worry yourself about it, my lord," she said. "You have been the host of this party and therefore your attentions have been engaged elsewhere."

"That is true," he said. "As you may know, I have been urged to court another young woman. I have found, however, that I cannot control what — or who — my heart longs for."

His conversation with Lady Hester would not be quite as truthful as that with Lady Diana.

Her eyes narrowed. "I have seen your private conversations with Lady Templeton."

"Lady Templeton?" he repeated, as if the thought had not occurred to him. "We are old friends, through the Duchess of Breckenridge."

"Ah, I heard that to be the case," she said, cautiously. "How well are you currently acquainted with the Duchess?"

"We were friends as children, but I have not spoken with her in ages," he said waving a hand, to which Lady Hester seemed relieved to hear. William knew the woman had tried to come between Olivia and her duke, and he imagined Lady Hester rather hoped he didn't know the details of the situation.

"So the woman you are so enamored with..." she began, and William smiled. Good. She had heard his conversation with Lady Diana, as he had planned.

"I must not speak of it here," he said, looking around him furtively. "Perhaps — would you meet me in the woods shortly? Just on the edge of the woodland, past the creek — do you know where I mean?"

"I do, my lord," she said, a sly grin crossing her face. She leaned toward him, purposefully showing him an ample amount of cleavage. "I shall see you shortly. Allow me to leave first."

"Absolutely," he said with a nod. As he watched her leave, he crossed the room to the servant's galley. "Roberts," he said to the man waiting. "It's time."

"Very good, my lord," said the man. "Also, Cook has prepared something for you, according to the wishes of Lady Templeton."

"Oh?" He asked, curious as he stepped into the room.

His man brought him over a tincture, "It smells rather strongly, my lord, would you like me to apply it as directed?"

"Might as well try, Roberts," he said, and the man used a handkerchief to apply it to his forehead and the back of his neck. William had to admit the smell wasn't altogether vile, and even on first sniff, it seemed to relax him somewhat.

"Thank you, Roberts," he said. "Now, on with it, man!"

"Very well," said Roberts, and quickly walked out the door to follow through with his portion of the plan.

"Ladies, gentlemen," William called out to gather the attention of his guests who were located in the adjoining rooms. They were not all present, some taking the time to prepare for the evening meal, the final one of the party, but there were still enough people to serve his purpose. "It is such a lovely afternoon. Might we take our refreshments outdoors and enjoy the fresh air?"

He saw a few quizzical looks, but Merryweather clapped his hands and told him what a fine idea it was, and the group followed him out the doors of the conservatory to the gardens beyond. William was pleased to see the parents of Lady Hester were following him, although they looked rather curious as to where their daughter may be.

They exited the house and gathered in the gardens, which were beginning to look somewhat more manicured under William's attention while still maintaining the natural charm. William tried to remain at ease, and he did have to admit that his headache was somewhat subsiding, a fact that shocked him, as nothing else had ever seemed to work. A flurry of color caught his eye, and he turned to see the woman he was looking for ascending the hill out of the woods.

"Lady Hester!" he said as the woman approached, a furious look on her face. Her eyes widened as she took in the group assembled in front of her. "And ... my, is that Lord Templeton?" The man crested the hill after Lady Hester, his face an equal mask of rage. He looked slightly worse for wear, which was to be expected after he had been stabbed with a knife, hit with a tree branch, and then held by William's steward for a couple of hours.

"Hester?" The woman's mother stood and approached. "Where have you been? And why were you with Lord Templeton — unchaperoned?"

"I was *not* with Lord Templeton!" Lady Hester cried. "At least, I didn't mean to be. Why, I was ... I was...." she looked over at William, who maintained a look of innocence on his face. She couldn't very well say she had gone into the woods to meet with another man, now could she? One who had remained at the house the entire time she had been gone.

"Lord Templeton?" Lady Hester's father rose now as the man approached. "What is the meaning of this? What were you doing with my daughter?"

"Your daughter? I was not ... that is to say I was in the woods because ... because," he looked around wildly, his true intentions, of course, nothing he could ever share with any other soul. "I was simply getting some air," he finished.

Hester's father did not seem to accept the story, shaking his head slowly as he looked from his daughter to the man.

"Hester, Lord Templeton," he said. "Perhaps we had best

discuss this inside. Lord Southam, may we have use of your library?"

"Of course," William said, opening the door to the house and leading them inside, not missing the furious glares bestowed upon him by both Lady Hester and Lord Templeton. Templeton had come here for a bride. Well, now he was going to find himself with one. William felt a twinge of guilt at what would, likely, be a lifetime of unhappiness for the two. And yet, he thought with a shrug, stranger things had happened. Perhaps they would find something with one another, an attachment that might make them happy. One never knew. They had worked hard to create unhappiness between others, however. Lady Hester had gleefully seized the opportunity to drive him and Rosalind apart when his brother had presented her with the note, despite the fact she knew Rosalind had not left the party — at least not willingly. And Templeton, well, he only wished there was more he could do to give the man the fate he deserved.

He turned back to the party, re-engaging with his guests. He saw both Merryweather and Lady Diana give him questioning looks as if they suspected something more at play, but of course nothing could ever, nor would ever, be proven. He smiled at them in return. The first part of his plan had been a success. Act two would begin shortly.

"To a happy future together!" William said in congratulations, raising his glass to the newly betrothed couple, who looked somewhat strained as waves of discomfort and perhaps a bit of embarrassment emanated from the pair. "May you find all you are looking for together."

He sat down, and his mother looked at him with

narrowed eyes, as if she knew he was up to something. He was aware that until Lord Templeton had emerged from the woods, she had thought the man was with Rosalind, hopefully quite far by now, and upon his return she seemed rather on edge. When Lady Southam had come downstairs to find the man in the drawing room, a look of shock had crossed her face, although she hid it rather quickly.

"Mother," he said, leaning over to her, aware that the rest of the table was fairly quiet. "Have you seen Lady Templeton this afternoon?"

"Lady Templeton?" she asked, raising her eyebrows. "I, ah, believe she ... left. I told you this, William, this afternoon."

"But did she?" he asked, and he could feel all of the eyes at the table on him.

"Of course," she said with a bit of a nervous laugh, her eyes flitting around the guests who had begun to stare. "In fact, she said something about returning home. I believe she had enough of the party."

"Did she tell you of this?" he asked, spearing a potato.

"She did," his mother said, grasping onto the out she had provided him. "We all know that Lady Templeton wasn't particularly ... fond of gatherings such as this, now was she?"

"That's interesting," said a voice from the doorway, and Rosalind walked into the room, taking her place at the empty seat that William had ensured his staff knew to place for her. "I do not recall such a conversation, Lady Southam."

"Oh, but it was just this morning," William's mother said quickly, trying to wave off Rosalind's words. "And where have you been all afternoon, then, Lady Templeton? I ... I was under the impression that you had decided to return to your betrothed."

"I have no betrothed, Lady Southam. And I was in my room," she said. "I was feeling rather ill, and so I decided to take to my bed."

"Ah," Lady Southam said, raising her wine glass to her lips. "I am so ... thrilled ... you are feeling better."

Rosalind smiled at her, and the guests murmured to one another in slightly softened tones, as if feeling the tension in the air, though no one was able to put any word to it.

William looked over at her, catching her eye and smiling at her. The ache in his head had eased, Lord Templeton didn't appear to be much of a problem anymore, and Rosalind ... well, Rosalind seemed to have found a strength within herself that William had been hoping she would come across in due time. There was only one thing keeping him from what he truly desired — to know of what feelings she held. Did she truly feel something for him, or had they simply come to be friendly with one another? He had to know ... and he wasn't sure how he would cope were her answer the latter.

26

Rosalind's heart beat wildly. On her way into the drawing room after dinner, Patty had slipped a note into her hand, and when she read it, she wasn't sure what to think.

Before you retire for the evening, meet me where we discovered your ability to swim. Do not bring company.—W

The hours had stretched intermediately long after she'd read William's missive, and she had worked herself into something of a state, unsure what William would have to say to her. Now that the danger seemed past them, what could he feel about her? It wasn't as if his mother and brother were gone from his life, and she didn't see how it would be possible to live under the same roof as them. And as truly awful as they were, she could never ask him to choose her over them. They were his family, his blood, and she knew that would still mean something to him.

She wished she was wearing boots as she trekked through the somewhat long grass that evening, but there had been no opportunity to return to her room after dinner.

The full moon lit her path to the small pond, and she heard the water before she saw anything.

"You came."

His voice, a husky baritone, cut through the sounds of the night air, and she turned to it, its warmth softening all of the tension she carried.

"Of course I did," she said, and he closed the distance between them, running his hands down her arms, leaving goose flesh in their wake, and not because of the temperature, for the evening was still warm.

"Rosalind," he said. "I am so sorry for all that has happened to you. So much has occurred that has seemed to keep us apart, and yet...."

"Here we are," she finished, looking up at him, at the way the moonlight played off his cheekbones, as his deep blue eyes, nearly black in the moonlight, looked down at her, turbulent in emotion. She wished she knew the thoughts and feelings behind them.

"I—"

"You—"

They started at the same time, and both laughed a little self-consciously.

"Perhaps," he said softly, "words are not the place to start."

He leaned in and kissed her then, his lips moving over hers slowly to begin, tasting her, as if asking a question. She responded, finding herself melting into him. At her apparent answer, his arms came around her, and as she felt the planes of his hard chest against her, and she sighed a little bit into his mouth. Here was a man she could live with, a man who was worthy of love, and who would, she now knew, treat her well. She had doubted she could ever trust another, but William had proven to her time and again that he believed in her, that he put her first, that he never wavered from who he was and who he had always been.

He finally broke the kiss, pulling back slightly as he looked at her, running the soft pads of his thumbs down the side of her face to her jawline.

"Rosalind," he breathed. "You are the loveliest thing I have ever seen in all my life."

She laughed a little. "I highly doubt that."

"No more of that," he said with a shake of his head, and Rosalind nodded. After all that had transpired over the past few days, she felt surer of herself than she ever had before. She knew she had to continue to believe in herself, that she deserved more of life than she had previously allowed herself, but changes were, quite often, slow to come. But come they did.

"Rosalind," he repeated, a serious countenance taking over his face. "I asked you this before, and you did not have an answer for me. So much has occurred since then, though it has been but a few days. I must, however, ask you again. Do you love me?"

She swallowed, looking down at her hands. Why must he ask her this? She would so prefer to know his own feelings first. To confess her love would be a risk she wasn't used to taking. And yet, she had vowed to herself that she would put her own happiness first and, as Tillie had told her, be true to her heart and where it led her. Whatever he said to her, whatever came of this conversation, she must know the truth.

"I do," she said in a whisper. "I am sorry I did not tell you so before, William, but I was scared. There is so much to be determined, and yet ... I find my thoughts full of nothing but you. I have hoped that you felt something of the same, although I could not be sure—"

"Oh, Rosalind," he said, his arms pulling her tighter to him. "I do not think I deserve you. I know what it means for you to say those words. I know what you have suffered in the past, how men have previously hurt you. To know that you can find room in your heart for me means more than I can explain."

"If there is anything I have learned, William, from these past weeks, it is that love is complicated," she said slowly, her eyes on the ground of the woods. "I have let so many other ideas, emotions, and thoughts go through my mind that I have not let my feelings guide me. What I had with Harold was nothing compared to what I have with you. You, William, are a good person. One who is kind, with a compassionate heart, but who has to deal with undeserved pain. Harold was ... well, Harold was an ass. And the greatest difference? The greatest difference is love. I love you, William, with all of my heart, and whatever comes with that, so be it. I promise to love you when you are happy and to love you when you are in pain. I will be there beside you, helping you through whatever comes. All I ask, William, is that you forgive me. I was a fool, pushing you away as I was overcome by my own insecurities to the extent that I missed how much you needed me. That will never happen again. I will expect your respect, it's true, but you need only to tell me what is wrong and we will deal with it together. I pushed you away, William, but I must ask you, will you ... will you have me still?"

"Will I have you?" he laughed his low, throaty chuckle, and she could practically see the tension escape him. "How is that even a question? You are everything I could have ever wanted. What I realize now is that before you, I didn't know what it meant to love. I thought I did, but that was not real love. That was a boy's infatuation. You are a woman who has stolen my heart, when I did not even know it was available to give. I am sorry if I have ever hurt you, in any way. I was a fool for not seeing you for so many years, but if you take me on, I will see you every day for the rest of our lives."

Her heart full at his words, she gazed up at him, feeling the smile stretch across her face.

"Marry me, Rosalind," he said, imploring her with his eyes. "Make me happier than I deserve to be, for the rest of my days."

"What of your family, William? They hate me," she said, lowering her gaze to his chest, but looking up suddenly when he snorted.

"They no longer matter," he said, shaking his head with a smile. "Only you do. My brother, he can make his own way now and his debts are his own. I have done enough for him. I will continue to look after my mother, but she is no longer welcome in my home. She can find a place for herself in London or perhaps — perhaps there is a cottage in the woods where she may make herself comfortable."

"Oh, William," Rosalind said with a laugh. "I am not sure that is a place for anyone to live, regardless of what they have done."

"We'll fix it up some," he said with a shrug. "I can hardly bear to think of what may have happened to you if you had not escaped from Templeton. You, Rosalind," he gave her a quick kiss on the forehead, "are a truly remarkable woman. I know you do not share yourself with most, so I feel ever so lucky to have truly discovered what a gift you are."

"I love you, William."

"And I you."

He leaned down then and kissed her, his lips full of both passion and promise as he drew her even closer, and her senses were filled with him, the taste of mint and brandy on his breath, his unique scent of masculinity that she could now recognize anywhere in her nostrils, the hard muscle beneath her fingers and the soft lips on hers.

Her fingers curled around his cravat, tugging it free from his shirt as she was desperate for more of the man that somehow, despite all that had tried to come between them was now suddenly, inexplicably — hers.

"Rosalind," he said, breaking away from her, his breathing ragged as he placed his forehead upon hers. "That may not be a good idea."

"Why ever not?"

"Because I want more of you — I want all of you. I have tasted your kiss but I want so much more, and if we begin down that path ... it will be so difficult to stop."

"You do not have to," she said, reaching up on her tiptoes to trail a hand down the side of his strong jaw. "I am no innocent virgin, William. I am not a wanton, true, and would never give myself to a man who I did not intend to spend the rest of my life with. But the love I feel for you now is more than I ever felt for the man I was married to, and the expression of that will be so much truer, have so much more meaning. Please, William, show me what love truly feels like."

He said nothing, but the look in his eyes imparted all that needed to be said. He claimed her lips once more, as her fingers worked at his cravat, now fully loosening it so she could slip her hands underneath to feel his chest upon her fingertips. He shook himself free of his jacket and bent to lay it on the soft grass underneath them. He swept her into his arms and gently laid her down upon it as he kneeled over top of her.

She pushed herself up to her knees, focusing on the man she loved illuminated by the moonlight behind him.

She tugged his shirttails free and he threw the garment over his head himself. She felt her jaw fall open at the sight of his broad, muscular chest, which was dusted with a sprinkle of tight, bronze curls. She reached out a hand to feel them, and he groaned when she found his flat nipples.

When Rosalind heard the noise escape his lips, she felt slightly powerful in her ability to make him feel as she did. He reached around her, gently untying the back of her dress until it was free to slip off of her shoulders. He reached down for the hem of her gown, and she pulled back, suddenly shy at him seeing her. She knew she didn't have much of a figure, didn't possess the sensuous curves that most men appreciated.

"Do not hide," he whispered. "I want to see you — all of you."

He gently dispensed of her dress, before pulling her chemise overhead. She felt the warm night air caress her, and she closed her eyes for a moment, unsure of what William would think. When she finally opened them, she found he was looking at her in wonder, a slight smile seemingly tugging at the corner of his mouth.

"You are absolutely beautiful," he whispered, and she felt tears in her eyes.

This was not her first time, true, but it certainly felt like it. Never before had her heart beat with such anticipation. Never before had she nearly lost her breath due to the beauty that was before her and for all the emotion she felt within her. Never before had she experienced such wonder, such emotion that she knew was fully returned.

He kissed her, and she moaned and reached her arms up around him as he trailed heat down the side of her neck with the gentle flutter of his lips. His head continued down, until he found the peak of one of her breasts, taking it into his mouth and suckling. Her hips bucked toward him, and he gently lowered her back down to the ground and his hand moved between her legs, finding her center with deft fingers.

She ran her hands through his hair, and he shifted his attention from one breast to the other. He slipped a finger inside her, and she felt a growing sensation deep within her, unlike anything she had ever felt before.

"William…." she murmured, and he lifted his head to look at her, though his fingers continued their ministrations.

"Are you all right?"

"I am … I am more than … oh, William…"

"Yes?" he asked, his voice hoarse as he was seemingly struggling to maintain control. Unsure of what she was doing, but compelled to do so all the same, Rosalind reached down between them, and instinctively began stroking her hand over the swell of the front of his trousers. He groaned and shifted away from her, and she momentarily felt the loss of his presence before she realized he was simply dispensing of the fabric that remained between them. He threw his pants into the growing pile of clothing, and her hand found his manhood. She explored the length of him, running his fingers over him before taking him in her fist, up and down, back and forth. William's head fell back and he arched into her, before his voice rasped out, "Rosalind, darling, that feels better than you know, but you need to stop — now."

She felt her desire growing at his words, at what she was able to do to him, and he shifted away from her, bracing himself atop her on his elbows. She brushed a drop of sweat away from his brow and reached her legs up to circle him. When he thrust deep inside of her, she threw her head back. He flexed his hips and began to move. It felt more perfect, more right than anything ever had before. He stroked long and deep, and Rosalind arched her hips up toward him, aching for something, though she wasn't entirely sure what. She had never before felt such an ache within her. She looked up at William, and his brow remained furrowed, as if in deep concentration. He thrust again and again and reached down a hand to stroke her.

"Come for me, love," he said, and suddenly everything shattered in an explosion that she couldn't have explained if she had tried.

27

William had never known it could feel like this — he had never known what it meant when the physical expression of love joined with the actual sentiment.

As he felt Rosalind find her release, he no longer held himself back, and he let go himself, feeling unparalleled satisfaction.

Finally, he collapsed on top of her, holding just enough of his weight off of her so as not to crush her.

"Oh, William," she finally said, her breath still coming quickly. "That was ... exquisite. I didn't know that it could be like that."

He pushed himself up on his palms and stared deeply into her eyes. The light through the trees cast shadows upon her face, but he could still see the sea green looking up at him, catching him and pulling him into their depths.

He felt her arms go round his back, and her fingernails stroked his sweat-dampened skin. He turned onto his side, bringing her with him so that her head was resting in the crook of his arm.

"Indeed it was," he said. His heart broke slightly at the thought of her being with another man, one who didn't take her own pleasure into account. He tried to push the thought from his mind, not wanting to ruin this moment with the idea of another with her, as difficult as it was. She was his now, and he would make sure she felt his love for the rest of their lives.

"I love you, Rosalind," he said, raising her hand to his mouth and kissing her wrist. She was so delicate, and yet he knew the strength within her, and he wanted to make sure she never forgot it either.

"And I you," she whispered.

He wasn't sure how long they lay there together under the moon and the stars, which shone down upon them with the music of nature all around. He smiled at the croak of the frogs, the wind whispering through the grass, and the chirp of the crickets. He reached over to their pile of clothing and found her gown, laying it overtop of them, though the night air was warm and comforting.

"Do you think we could stay out here all night?" she asked sleepily, and he smiled at her question.

"We could, I suppose," he said. "We could scandalize everyone and come in just in time to greet the guests for their final breakfast before they leave. It wouldn't much bother me, would it you?"

She laughed. "I'm not sure. Probably."

"I know," he said, planting a kiss on her forehead. "Which is why we will go in shortly."

"William ... you do know I may never be the hostess a man like you needs as a wife?"

"Rosalind," he said firmly, "It matters naught to me what type of hostess you are. Will we attend the odd social function? Yes. But you can be whoever you want there. I expect nothing of you. And if we have guests and you choose to hide away in the library with a book, then so be it. I can entertain guests. But I cannot find another woman who would make me as happy as you, who I would so desire for a wife. And therefore everything else is secondary."

He leaned up on his elbow so she could see the seriousness on his face. "Do you understand? No more talk of you being unworthy, because that is so far from the truth."

She nodded. "Understood, my lord."

He laughed then and eased himself back down. He was fortunate to know her, let alone to have her. He vowed he would spend the rest of his days making sure she was fully aware of that.

It was shortly before dawn when Rosalind and William snuck back into the house. Rosalind felt it was as though an air of joy surrounded them. She almost didn't want to acknowledge it, for fear that it would disappear. She had never known such happiness, such peace, such contentment, and she was fearful that it wouldn't last.

And yet when she woke after an hour of sleep, it was still there, a feeling that had settled deep within her heart. Could it be? She thought to herself. Was this a true, lasting happiness?

When she joined the party for breakfast, she found that Alfred and Lady Southam were conspicuously absent. William had asked her the night before if she wanted their betrothal announced to the party, and she had shaken her head. She would prefer to tell people on their own, and not have a grand announcement. He had agreed, telling her he would do as she wished, and she was pleased he had acknowledged her sentiments, though she couldn't help but meet his eye time and again as he looked down the table toward her.

Fortunately, much of the attention was kept from them and directed toward Lord Templeton and Lady Hester. They seemed wary of one another, although there did seem to be somewhat of an understanding between them, Rosalind noted. Who knew? Perhaps they would find happiness with one another or at the very least an understanding that they would never have found with any other. And if they were both bent on making their spouse unhappy, well then, it was best they do so for one another than to an otherwise unsuspecting soul. She knew she should feel guilty about forcing the two of them together — she knew William did. And yet, after all that Hester had done to Olivia, all that she had said to her, Rosalind couldn't help but feel slightly pleased about the whole thing.

"Isn't it lovely?" Anne leaned over and whispered to her with a grin. She was well aware of how Hester had tried to come between her brother and his wife. "I know he is your brother-in-law, Rosalind, but I hope the man is truly awful to her!"

Rosalind tried not to laugh at Anne's vehemence. The girl was not one to cross, that was for certain.

William thanked everyone for joining them, wishing them all safe travels and adieu. As the guests began filtering out of the room, Tillie drew Rosalind to the side.

"Am I to suppose from the way you and Lord Southam were practically eating one another for breakfast that all has been resolved between the two of you?" Her eyebrow quirked upward in a way that made Rosalind laugh.

"I suppose you could say that," she said, feeling warmth creep up her cheeks.

"I am glad," the Duchess responded. "I had a suspicion that all would work out well for you. No great love story is without its perils. For it is the only way one can truly appreciate the resulting happiness."

"I suppose you are right, Tillie," said Rosalind, then surprised herself as well as the Duchess when she reached her arms out in an embrace. "I am so happy to have gotten to know you. I hope we can renew our acquaintance soon."

"Absolutely," said Tillie with a wide grin. "I would love that. Until then."

She nodded her head and sailed out of the room, with Rosalind smiling after her. What a week it had been, she thought, then suddenly she felt strong arms encircle her waist, and William nuzzled her neck.

"I suppose I best get to securing a marriage license, should I not?" he asked, his voice low and husky.

"I suppose you should," she said, turning in his arms to reach her hands around his neck. "Oh William, could you ever have imagined that after everything we've been through, this is where we would end up?"

"I have quite the imagination, so I have to say that yes, I could see it," he said with a teasing grin, and she swatted him before growing serious.

"I have no dowry to offer you," she said. "Will that matter?"

"Not at all," he said, encircling her in his arms. "I have business prospects that I believe will soon come to fruition, and I also will no longer be supporting my brother. Roberts informed me that Alfred has already departed, apparently now finally concerned that his actions may come to light. I promise you, Rosalind, he will never set foot in this house again."

"Thank you for that, William," she said. "Though he is

still your brother. While I do not entirely feel safe with him about, perhaps you shouldn't completely be estranged from him. He will always be part of your family."

"You are kinder than any woman I have ever known," he said, planting a kiss on her lips. "We shall see what comes. Perhaps if Alfred proves himself in time, I can somewhat forgive him, although I shall never, ever forget what he has done. Now, come, I have something for you. Consider it an early wedding gift."

She raised her eyebrows as she looked up at him, but nodded in agreement as he led her out the door and across the yard.

As they approached the stable, she smiled, knowing, hoping for what they were here.

Friday greeted them when they entered the door of the stable, yapping excitedly as he led them over to his family. She knelt beside the puppies, who seemed to have already grown in just a few short days. She ran her hands over them, the four who played together, and the fifth who lay on her own, contentedly snuggled into her mother's side.

"I am not sure if they will end up going back to the neighbor's or staying here," William said. "They all have their run of the land of course. But I thought, perhaps, there might be one you'd like to keep as your own. I was going to pick one for you, but I thought it might be best to see which one you'd prefer."

"Which one were you going to choose?" she asked, looking up at him.

"That one," he said, pointing to the lone puppy, and she was surprised to see his face turn slightly pink over his collar. "I know it seems silly, but there is something about her that reminds me of you. Not that you're alone, per se, but she's quiet and somewhat timid, and yet, she loves her mother and when she feels like it, she plays just fine. Does that seem foolish?"

"Not at all," she said, scooping up the puppy and rising to her feet. "You were exactly right." She leaned up on her tiptoes and kissed him, and he smiled at her, tucking a strand of hair behind her ear.

"Rosalind," he said with a bit of a sigh. "I am not really sure what to do now, in the immediate future. I realize you're not an innocent debutante but to stay here alone, unwed, it is rather scandalous. Does that ... bother you?"

"Not really," she said with a shrug. "I have learned that what others may think of me does not determine whether or not I shall be happy. Does it matter to you?"

"No," he said. "But I do want to do right by you. I have an idea. It's a bit of an impetuous one, I must admit."

"Yes?" she said, raising an eyebrow at him.

"Have you heard of a place called Gretna Green?"

She laughed at that. "William! You want to run away to marry in Scotland like scandalous young lovers?"

"Why not?" he asked with a laugh. "We're somewhat scandalous, we are somewhat young, and we are somewhat lovers. It would be an adventure, would it not?"

"You are right," she said, feeling the grin stretch across her face. "It would be an adventure."

They smiled at one another, and Rosalind thought her heart might burst out of her chest for the amount of love it now held.

EPILOGUE

ne Year Later

THE SUN PEEKED over the horizon as the old rocker creaked back and forth where William had placed it behind the house overlooking the garden and the meadow beyond. Rosalind hummed a low tune as she ran her hand over the baby's back, her dog, Flora, sleeping at her feet.

As the baby nuzzled into her chest, Rosalind sighed. She had never, ever thought it would be possible to feel such contentment. After Harold had died, she would have been happy with a small cottage and a dog to share her life with. Now, she had the dog, true, but so much more than she had never dreamed to be possible — a beautiful home in the English countryside, a child snuggled in her arms, and a husband to spend the rest of her life with, who would love and cherish her with all he was.

She heard his footsteps approaching from behind her,

and felt William lean down and kiss the top of her head as he lay a thin quilt over the two of them. She didn't really need it, not with the warm sun upon them, but all the same it was a lovely gesture that she certainly wouldn't turn away.

He pulled up a chair beside her, and Rosalind tried not to laugh at how hard he was trying to be silent, though he was failing miserably. Fortunately, the baby was sleeping soundly and didn't even twitch at his efforts.

Rosalind smiled when she recalled their wedding. It was just the two of them at the Scottish border, and the old priest had smiled at the love evident on their faces. As a compromise to their friends who had pestered them so about running off to be married alone, they had held a ball celebrating their union. It was still a rather small affair, with just their closest acquaintances, and Rosalind had found it incredibly lovely. William had danced with her the entire night, not caring about propriety, and there was nothing but love in the room.

Despite how much she knew her husband felt for her, she had some slight trepidations about his reaction upon seeing Olivia. Would he still feel something for her? Was a flicker of his former infatuation still there? Yet there had been nothing but the pleasure of seeing an old friend.

Rosalind had been both elated and relieved when she found out she was with child. It was a dream she had given up on, and yet had been made a reality after she had found love with William.

Of course she loved William with all of her heart, but she had never known what love could truly feel like until she had held her babe in her arms. She knew her mother would be horrified if she knew how Rosalind was raising the child. For she hadn't hired a nursemaid, as was the practice of most women of the *ton*. She had no desire to go to

London and attend the social functions of the season, and therefore decided to raise the child, to nurse him herself. And what her mother thought, well, Rosalind didn't really care. She had written her mother to tell her of her marriage, as well as the baby, and she received a congratulatory note. Rosalind wasn't quite ready to invite her parents to visit, but in time she would. She wasn't one to live with that type of animosity in her life, and she needed to mend the rift between her and her parents, despite all they had done or tried to do.

"I have a surprise for you," William whispered in her ear. "A package arrived."

He slipped the leather-bound volume into her hands, and she tried not to start with the joy that overcame her. It was a book — *her* book. A publisher had accepted her manuscript, and here it was, in printed copy. A tear fell from her eye as she sat back, overcome.

She didn't know what else the future held for her, for William, for their child or children to come, but, with William's help, she was beginning to learn that there was no point in worrying.

No, the most important thing was to find happiness, and be grateful for every moment of it. She appreciated the sunsets. She treasured the animals that filled their life with excitement. And most of all, she cherished her family, and the man who had made it happen.

"I love you, William," she whispered, leaning her head back to look at him.

He wrapped an arm around her. "And I love you."

THE DUKE SHE WISHED FOR

HAPPILY EVER AFTER BOOK 1

PREVIEW

Read the story of Tabitha and Nicholas...

CHAPTER 1

Tabitha heard the opening creak of the front door of the shop float through past the heavy curtains that separated her workshop from the sales floor. She tensed over the silk ribbon she was attempting to fashion into a flower shape and waited for the sound of her stepsister Frances to greet whomever had just walked into the Blackmore Milliner shop.

She paused, waiting a little bit longer before pushing out a frustrated breath and standing. These velvet ribbon flowers she had learned to fashion were part of the reason Blackmore hats sat atop some of the finest female heads in polite society—she had a knack for creating new ways to adorn the same old bonnet or beaver hat styles so that a woman of a certain class stood out among her peers.

This ability was both a blessing and a curse, it turned out. Her creativity meant Tabitha brought customers through the front door, to the shop she and her father had built after her mother died when she was seven years old. It had brought Tabitha and her father, the baronet Elias Blackmore, closer together in their time of immeasurable grief and the shop had flourished.

The relationship between father and daughter was so strong, that when he approached her when she was 12 to tell her he wanted to marry a baroness from the north country who had a daughter about her own age, Tabitha had been happy for her father and excited to have a sister. She had welcomed her new family with an open heart and open arms.

What a silly little fool she'd been, Tabitha thought to herself with derisive snort as she pushed herself to her feet and through the brocade curtains to greet the newcomer. Lord only knew where Frances had gone off to. Likely shopping with her mother, Ellora.

Upon the untimely death of Sir Elias Blackmore three years after the marriage, Tabitha had been utterly devastated. Lady Blackmore, however, hadn't wasted much time in putting Tabitha in her place. No longer the family's most cherished daughter, Tabitha had been shoved into the workroom and largely ignored. The more she stood up to Ellora, the more her stepmother threatened to throw her out on the street. Knowing it was within Ellora's nature to follow through on her threat, Tabitha did her best to ignore and avoid her stepmother, focusing instead on her work and her ambitions.

It was better, Tabitha supposed, than staying in their townhome all day long worrying about social calls that never came or invitations that would never arrive. The family name had suffered greatly under Lady Blackmore and Miss Frances Denner, her daughter from a previous marriage.

In truth, Tabitha was little more than a servant with no money to speak of, no family to lean on, and no real prospects other than her creations on which to pin her hopes of ever escaping the lot she'd been given after her father died.

In the showroom, Tabitha scanned the floor in search of the new arrival. It took a moment, but her eyes finally landed on a small, older man in a fine suit. He had a slip of paper in his hand and he approached Tabitha with the air of someone who didn't waste time.

"Good afternoon, Miss," the man began with perfect, practiced speech. "My name is Mr. McEwan. I serve as the steward in the house of Her Grace the Duchess of Stowe. I have a receipt for a series of hats I believe she had ordered and requested that they be delivered tomorrow afternoon."

Tabitha felt her stomach sink. If this was the order of which she was thinking, the one currently on her worktable, there was no way under the stars that the three hats would be ready by tomorrow. She was only one flower (out of seven) into the first bonnet and it was a slow process to convince the requested velvet ribbon to behave.

"I am sorry, sir," she began, trying to get his eyes off the wilder ostrich-plumed hats next to her and back on her. "That is almost four days before we agreed upon. I'm certain there is no feasible way the work can be done, and done well, by tomorrow."

That got the older man's attention. He huffed, turned a bit pink around the cheeks, and sputtered.

"There is simply no choice, my dear," he said abruptly but not unkindly. "His Grace is arriving home from his trip to France early and therefore the parties his mother has planned for him will be adjusted accordingly. And so, her wardrobe *must* be ready—she said so herself. She is willing to pay handsomely for your ability to expedite the process."

Tabitha drew in a breath at that and considered. She

was having such a difficult time scrimping a small savings together to buy herself a seat at the Paris School of Millinery that this "bonus" money might perhaps get her there that much quicker. Assuming, of course, that Ellora didn't catch wind of the extra earnings. She was quick to snatch up all but the barest pennies.

Tabitha closed her eyes for a moment and drew a steadying breath. If she worked through the night and her needle and thread held true, there was a *slight* chance that she could finish in time. She said so to Mr. McEwan, who beamed brightly at her.

"I knew it," he said with a laugh. "I have faith you Miss—er, I apologize, I did not hear your name?"

Tabitha sighed.

"Tabitha Blackmore," she said, noticing how quickly he'd changed the subject on her. "I did not exactly say that I would be able to—"

She was cut off again by Mr. McEwan, who gave her a slight bow and provided directions to the home of the Dowager Duchess of Stowe on the other side of the city.

"I shall see you tomorrow, then, my dear," he said with a quick grin. "Be sure to pack a bag to stay at least one evening, maybe two. I am certain Her Grace's attendants will need proper coaching on how best to pair the hats. You will be paid, of course!"

With that the short man with wisps of white hair on his head that stood up like smoke was gone, disappearing into the streets of Cheapside.

Tabitha leaned back against the counter behind her and blew out a breath, a little overwhelmed at the entire encounter.

On the one hand, she had found a way to increase her savings and take a step closer to the education her father had wanted for her. On the other, getting through the night in one piece was not guaranteed. She would have to return to the shop after dinner and do so without rousing Lady Blackmore's suspicions, which would not be easy.

Tabitha kicked at a crushed crepe paper flower that hadn't been tossed out properly. Another evening down the back drainpipe it was then.

"Time away from the witch, I suppose," she muttered as she returned to her worktable, a new fire of inspiration lit beneath her.

Dinner was more complicated than usual, thanks to the fact that Ellora, Tabitha's stepmother, was having one of her *moods.* They could be brought on by anything—the weather (too foul or too pleasant), the noisy street they lived on, memories of her life when she was the daughter of an earl and had endless opportunities for money and titles, or even an egg that had too much salt.

Today's mood, however, had more to do with the fact that her daughter Frances had been recently snubbed. Officially, Ellora was considered a member of the *ton* and her daughter's first season the previous year had nearly cost them the roof over their heads. However, Frances was an ill-tempered, sharp-tongued girl who did little to ensure repeat invitations to dances and parties.

"A true-and-true witch," their housekeeper, Alice, called her. Alice was the only servant left on staff besides Katie, the lady's maid Ellora and Frances shared, so it was up to both Alice and Tabitha to make sure that meals were made and rooms were kept clean. Being an indentured servant in her own home was trying enough, but much worse was having to tidy the room that once held every memento of her father's. It was now completely devoid of every memory of him.

It was as though Baronet Elias Blackmore had never existed. No portraits. No personal belongings. Nothing but the small locket he'd given Tabitha when she was nine years old and still wore around her neck.

This evening's dinner was a morose affair and Tabitha sat silently while Ellora ranted and raved about the social snub of her angel Frances.

Tabitha looked across the table at her stepsister. Frances was very pretty, she'd give her that much. But her mouth was drawn thin and her blue eyes were more steely than pleasant. Frances had brown hair that one could call more dishwater than brunette. However, Ellora spent high sums of money on beauty products and bits and bobs for Katie to fashion Frances' hair into something resembling high fashion each day.

Frances was pouting into her soup while her mother railed beside her. When she glanced up and caught Tabitha looking at her, she scowled.

Tabitha quickly looked away, but Frances jumped on the opportunity to take the attention off her.

"I saw a servant go into the shop this afternoon when I was returning from tea with Adela," Frances said to her mother, her flinty eyes on Tabitha, who inwardly groaned.

So much for secrecy.

Ellora paused in her ranting and raised an eyebrow at her.

"Who was it?"

The words were clipped and her nose was high in the air while she peered down her nose at Tabitha.

"A servant for the Dowager Duchess of Stowe," Tabitha

replied. "He came to inquire about an order the Duchess sent over a week ago."

It wasn't exactly a lie and it helped her corroborate her story because Ellora had already received the money sent over for the original order.

"And was the order ready?"

Tabitha swallowed hard. She wasn't in the clear yet.

"Almost," she said and lowered her eyes to take a sip of the soup as she inwardly seethed.

"Unacceptable," her stepmother ground out between her teeth. "You lazy, no-good hanger-on. It is no wonder your father's ridiculous hat shop is dying off. He had the laziest cow this side of the river working behind the curtains."

She banged a fist on the table, making Frances jump.

"You get up from this table and you finish that order right this instant," Ellora pointed a long bony finger in the direction of the door, ending Tabitha's dinner before she had progressed past the soup. Tabitha's stomach rumbled in protest, and her fists clenched beneath the table as she longed to tell Ellora what she really thought, but Tabitha knew this was a gift. She would nab a roll from Alice later.

"I am going to stop by in the morning to check your ledger and work progress to make certain you are being completely honest with me," Ellora announced. "And woe be to you if I find that you have been neglecting your work and you have a backlog of orders."

In reality, Tabitha was of legal age and the threats should be harmless. But she was also lacking any real money, any job prospects, and no titles her father could have passed down to her. Running her father's milliner shop was the closest thing she would have to freedom for the near future and it would be much better for her if she allowed Ellora the illusion of control for the time being, since the dreadful woman had inherited the shop upon her father's death.

Ellora's threat put Tabitha in a bind. She was due at the Duchess' estate first thing in the morning. As it stood, she'd have to have those pieces done, as well as the other orders on her workbench. She closed her eyes and blew out a heavy breath.

It was going to be a very long night.

CHAPTER 2

"You cannot go looking like that."

Tabitha rolled her eyes at her best friend's words. Matilda "Tillie" Andrews was the third child of one of England's most successful export and import families and the two young women had known each other since Sir Elias began importing millinery supplies with Captain Maximus Andrews. She was currently perched on the edge of Tabitha's work table.

Tillie, in her own right, was quite the seamstress and worked anonymously for a few of Cheapside's finer fashion houses designing party dresses that had been the talk of the season the past two years. She did not need to work, not like Tabitha, but she loved it. Tabitha thought she might also love her work more as well if she wasn't scrimping and saving for each and every single penny she could get her fingers on.

"I have to go like this," Tabitha said through a yawn. She had stayed up until sunrise finishing all of the Duchess's ornamentation. On top of that, she had four other pieces to assemble to beat Ellora's mid-morning arrival. She was exhausted and had unbecoming dark circles under her eyes, but she had finished with not a moment to spare.

"I have something I was going to show you," Tillie said, pulling her bag out and unfurling a gorgeous walking dress in the deepest shade of emerald.

Tabitha's mouth dropped open at the craftsmanship.

"Tillie," she breathed. "It's beautiful."

Her friend beamed.

"It's for Rochester's," she said with a shrug. "It's a sample, of course, but it does not need to be there for three days. So, you can wear it today and we will make sure you do not arrive on their doorstep looking like some sort of creature that crawled from the gutter."

Tabitha frowned and looked down on her drab, worn muslin gown. It wasn't *that* bad, was it?

"What are you doing this morning?" Tabitha asked as Tillie pushed her behind the work curtain of the shop and practically forced her to change her dress.

"Nothing," Tillie called. "Waiting for you to invite me along."

Tabitha stuck her head out between the curtains and smiled.

"I assumed you would be too busy," she said. "Would you like to go? It's a bit of a walk."

It was true. The townhouse owned by the Fairchild family was on the far side of town and not an easy walk.

"I have my father's chaise," Tillie replied. "I shall have our groom drive us."

"You drove?" Tabitha asked, looking toward the window. "I didn't see the carriage or the groom."

Tillie shook her head.

"He's getting himself something to eat a few streets away and watered the horses at Denton's," Tillie said. "Neither of us wanted to see your stepmother this morning, so we thought it best."

It was a good idea, Tabitha mused, appreciative of how very smart her best friend was. Ellora, while somewhat polite to Tillie's face, was an opportunist and cornered her friend for information about her eligible older brothers and cousins whenever she was around. Not that Tillie couldn't handle her, but Tabitha shuddered at one of those poor Andrews boys getting shackled with a crow like Frances.

"Are you quite ready?" Tillie asked in a huff, never one for patience. "I am absolutely starving and I want to stop for the small cakes at Lodge and Stone. They're my favorite, you know."

Oh, yes. Tabitha knew. Tillie was a connoisseur of delicious food, though you wouldn't be able to tell from the looks of her. She managed to maintain just the right curves in just the right places and was never shy about enjoying herself.

As well she should, Tabitha thought with a smile. Life was hard enough as it was, why not take a little joy where you could find it?

"I believe so," Tabitha said, suddenly shy at the form-fitting walking dress. It hugged her small body in the right places, more so than any of her ordinary dresses. And the color — it made her violet eyes simply shine in the full-length mirror before her. There were buttons and ribbons accenting the dress perfectly — not too many and not too few. She looked polished. Poised. So far from the normal, bedraggled mess that she was most other days that she pinched her cheeks for a little dash of color and smiled at her reflection.

"It's absolutely lovely," Tabitha breathed as Tillie came to stand behind her. Tabitha studied the hat displays in the shop and moved toward the back to find the perfect bonnet to complete the look, large peacock plume and all. She set it on top of the tawny locks piled on top of her head.

"Now we are ready."

Tabitha and Tillie left the shop and Tabitha locked the door behind her.

They walked the two long blocks to Denton's, a stabling station for people who could afford it. When the carriage was ready, Tillie and Tabitha climbed in and enjoyed the long ride toward the grand manse of the former Duke of Stowe, Reginald Fairchild. The Duke had died unexpectedly almost two years prior and his wife, the Dowager Duchess Gemma Fairchild, was slowly coming back out into polite society. As such, she found her wardrobe to be a bit outdated and on a recommendation her lady's maid had found her way into Tabitha's shop for the first time two months ago for a simple hat, which had turned into the most recent repeat order.

Nearly an hour later, they rolled to a stop in front of the Fairchild home and Tabitha sucked a breath through her lips.

"My goodness," she said as Tillie laughed beside her.

"You have that right," her friend replied.

The home was large, bedecked in white marble, and had four giant marble columns across the front of it. There was a small pond in the middle of the circle drive they took around to the back door. Tabitha counted an army of gardeners toiling away in preparation for what was likely going to be a few days' worth of guests and revelry.

When they were greeted by a footman, Tabitha gave her name and asked for Mr. McEwan. They waited a few brief moments before the older gentleman appeared and showed them inside.

Tabitha tried to keep pace with the steward as he led them down the long corridor.

"Very kind of you to make this happen, Miss Blackmore," the man said as he practically sprinted with his short, quick strides down a long hallway toward the back of the house. They stayed with him until he turned down a short hall.

"There now," he said, as he pushed the first door open to reveal a small office. "They are here, darling. Just like I said they would be."

"Darling" turned out to be a smartly dressed woman with an ample bosom, bright cheeks, and kind green eyes. She looked to be somewhere in her 50s and from the warm smile she gave Mr. McEwan, Tabitha guess they were about to meet *Mrs.* McEwan.

"Miss Tabitha Blackmore and Miss — my apologies," Mr. McEwan looked flustered as he glanced at Tillie, who whispered her name good naturedly to him. "Miss Matilda Andrews. This is my wife, Lorna McEwan, the housekeeper here. I leave you with her as we have quite a few preparations we are overseeing. His Grace is due to arrive at any moment."

The steward flittered away, leaving Tabitha and Tillie standing in the doorway, feeling awkward. Lorna had a warm smile as she rounded the desk she'd been sitting behind and led them down the hall to what looked like a simple dining room housing a long table and chairs. She took some of the boxes from Tabitha and put them down on the table.

"I was looking over a few of the accounts for Her Grace," the woman muttered in a thick brogue. "But now, this is exciting. This is one of her first hosted parties since His

Grace passed away and I know she is very nervous about the whole thing."

Mrs. McEwan began pulling the hats and fascinators from the box and tittering and clucking in appreciation.

"I knew you'd come through for us, Miss Blackmore," she said, mostly to herself. "You came highly recommended from Baron Wellesley's daughters and I knew you would provide the best for Her Grace."

Tabitha blushed a little and Tillie pinched her lightly in the side at the compliments.

"Are you her assistant?" Mrs. McEwan asked Tillie, who simply shook her head.

"She is a talented dressmaker," Tabitha blurted out before she could think better of it. She heard Tillie gasp at her secret identity being outed so quickly, but Lorna didn't look at all disapproving. In fact, she looked interested, so Tabitha pointed to the dress she was currently wearing.

"This is one of hers," she said, proud of her friend. "It is going to be a sample at Rochester's but she insisted I wear it to deliver these."

Mrs. McEwan gave the gown a steady gaze and smiled at her friend.

"You're very talented, Miss."

As Tillie was thanking her for the compliment, the door burst open with a train of three maids carrying two gowns each. Mrs. McEwan instructed them to hang the dresses on hooks along one side of the wall.

Six exquisite gowns were suddenly on display and she watched as Tillie took them all in, silently regarding every last detail on each one.

Mrs. McEwan stayed quiet a moment before speaking.

"So," she prodded. "Professional opinion, ladies?"

With the hats on the table in front of the gowns, Tabitha

realized what Lorna was asking. She wanted to know how they thought the gowns and the headwear matched up. As the last maid shut the door and left, Lorna looked to the ladies a second time.

"Well?"

After a moment of hesitation, both Tabitha and Tillie set upon the dresses and accessories, moving the feathers and ribbons around so that they paired up with the best gown. The housekeeper stepped back and watched as the two of them discussed ribbon shades and the texture of lace next to bright, fluffy feather plumes. When they were done, Lorna stepped forward, her eyes fixed on the ensembles they had put together with a smile on her face.

"Exquisite," she said reverently. "Absolutely exquisite. Do you happen to be free over the next two days?"

She turned toward them as she asked.

Tabitha didn't answer immediately, but Tillie did.

"I am supposed to leave with my mother in the morning for two weeks in Bath," she said. "I'm actually running behind schedule as it is. We are dining with my uncle at his club in a few hours."

Mrs. McEwan turned to Tabitha.

"I am not sure," she answered honestly. "I am not certain of what you are asking me right now?"

Mrs. McEwan cast a glance toward the gowns.

"The next few weeks are important to Her Grace for many, many reasons," she began. "First, she is venturing out of mourning and the eyes of her peers and contemporaries will be more than critical as she begins to immerse herself in the activities surrounding the season. I want her to shine, to put it bluntly, and none of her maids know a thing about dressing her to her station."

Tabitha could understand that. A duchess was expected

to have an air of regality that none beyond the royal family would possess.

"What's more," the woman continued. "Her son is expected to return this season and select a wife, so all eyes will be on His Grace as he moves through these parties and balls with an eye on the crowd for the next Duchess of Stowe."

Tabitha had heard rumors of Nicholas Fairchild, the latest Duke of Stowe. He was rumored to be a good-looking man who'd run wild in his younger days as the privileged sons of the elite were wont to do. He had managed to leave for France last year without a scandal chasing him out of town and as far as she understood, there wasn't one from the Continent chasing him back into town.

Either he was a well-behaved son of a duke or a very crafty duke who knew how to hide his indiscretions.

Whatever the case may be, as the daughter of a merchant baronet, the duke was so very far out of her realm that he might as well have existed in an alternate universe. Tabitha was a realist if nothing else, and spent very little time as a girl reading about white knights and rescues. She was a woman making plans to rescue herself.

"What I'm offering," Mrs. McEwan continued, pulling Tabitha back from her thoughts. "Is to pay for your services if you would agree to stay until tomorrow and make sure that the maids have Her Grace looking ravishing and heads above the rest. We need personal touches that it seems only the two of you can give. We shall pay you for your troubles. Handsomely."

Well, that did it. Handsomely, from the family of a duke, usually did mean *handsomely*, and that was money she needed to fund her schooling in Paris.

"I can do it," Tabitha said quickly, before she could

change her mind. "I just need to send a message, letting my stepmother know I will no longer return until tomorrow evening."

Crafting an expeditious white lie, Tabitha sent word to her stepmother that she was visiting with Tillie's family for the evening and would be back for supper the following day.

The games were surely afoot now, Tabitha thought to herself as she allowed Mrs. McEwan to show Tillie out and to lead her to her temporary rooms.

The Duke She Wished For is now available for purchase on Amazon, and is free to read through Kindle Unlimited.

QUEST OF HONOR

SEARCHING HEARTS BOOK 1

PREVIEW

Begin the stories of the Harrington family with Thomas and Eleanor...

PROLOGUE

Marie looked around the table at her five children, her gaze coming to rest on Thomas. Normally she was most concerned about Daniel, her eldest and the next in line to become Duke, but there was something about Thomas tonight that seemed off to her.

Typically the most free-spirited of her children, this evening he wore a serious look, and had taken on the brooding silence that overcame him whenever he felt stifled or frustrated.

The remainder of her children, from Daniel at 24 down to her 16-year-old daughter Polly, were chattering away as they were normally wont to do, no matter how she tried to instil in them the proper etiquette of the dinner hour. Her husband, Lionel, Duke of Ware, sat in his usual place at the head of the table, intent on his food as he listened to the stories of his brood.

"Thomas," Marie said, and he raised his dark head. "Is everything quite well, darling?"

"Yes, Mother," he replied mechanically.

"Are you quite sure?"

"Well actually," he said, looking hesitantly at her and then his father. "I do have somewhat of an announcement."

Marie raised her eyebrows as the chatter around the table hushed, for Thomas' siblings could see the nervousness that accompanied his statement.

"I am going to be joining the Navy," he said, puffing his chest out, trying to look more assured than he felt.

"The Navy!" his mother exclaimed incredulously. "You cannot be serious. Is this some sort of joke?"

"Not at all, Mother," he responded, his blue eyes taking on an icy resolve. "The Navy is a noble profession. What else am I to do with my life?"

"You are the second son of a Duke! What if the title of Duke should need to pass onto you and you are injured or dead somewhere at sea?"

"I shall not spend my life sitting here waiting for Father and Daniel to die, Mother," he responded, his voice becoming slightly more heated, although he would never raise it at his mother. "They are both quite healthy and, I'm sure, have long lives to live. I want to see the world! What better way than on the sea?"

"Lionel!" Marie said to her husband with fervour. "Have you nothing to say?"

Lionel finished chewing his potatoes, his expression unwavering.

"Well, son," he said. "I would say your intentions are admirable. You do know what you are getting yourself into?"

"I do."

"Well, then, boy, I'd best talk to my friend the Admiral tomorrow. The son of the Duke of Ware must find a reasonable berth and vessel upon which to serve."

Thomas' face lit up, and he caught the gaze of his sister

Violet, who smiled at him encouragingly. He grinned at her, then turned back to his father.

"Thank you, Father," he said. "I would appreciate it."

"This is quite ridiculous," his mother said, her head swivelling from Thomas to Lionel and back to Thomas once more. "Thomas is 22 years old! He and Daniel should be finding wives, settling down, raising children. Instead, Daniel is out doing Heaven knows what and Thomas will be at sea miles away from Britain! How is it that I have three children of marriageable age, none of which have any interest in actually being married?"

Benjamin and Polly smirked, happy to have the attention off of them and onto their three elder siblings.

"In due time, Mother," said Violet, somewhat mollifying her. "In due time. In the meantime, let us drink to Thomas and the world that awaits him."

"To Thomas!" They all joined in, with the exception of Marie, and Thomas grinned, excited about what the future would hold for him.

1

Five years later

Eleanor Adams sat primly on the straight backed chair as her father stomped around, muttering something under his breath. She waited patiently for his judgement to fall, knowing that he would not be able to bring himself to punish her too severely. After all, she was his only child and he had never been able to be too strict with her. In fact, this was the only life Eleanor had ever known. Just her and her father, facing the world and all its tribulations.

"You cannot simply do as you please, Eleanor!" her father spluttered, his face now a beetroot red. "What if we had not seen you?"

Eleanor stifled a sigh of frustration. "Papa, you know me better than that. I simply *had* to investigate whatever it was down there." A small smile crept across her face. "And, if I had not, then we would currently not have these three small trunks in our possession." She indicated the three, still damp, trunks that sat beside her father's desk, glancing at them before returning her gaze to her father.

To her very great relief, he sighed and sat down heavily, although he continued to shake his head at her. Eleanor hid her smile. She was triumphant.

"We have not opened them yet, Eleanor," her father said, a little gruffly. "You could have risked your life for nothing."

In response, Eleanor tossed her head, aware of the spots of moisture that shook off her long flaxen locks. "I am one of the best swimmers among the crew, Papa, you know that."

"But still," he retorted. "You cannot just dive off the ship without alerting someone to what you have found! Had you done so, I could have dropped the anchor and gone to see what was there."

Eleanor bit her lip, aware that her father was being more than reasonable. Had any one of his crew done what she had, they would have been severely punished. It was only because she was the captain's daughter that she had done such a thing. Her cheeks warmed. "I was trying to prove myself, Papa," she explained, more quietly. "As the only woman on board, I have to take extra steps to show my worth."

His face softened. "Eleanor, you already have my respect and the respect of the crew. For over twenty years you have traveled the seas with us and you have no need to prove yourself. Doing such a thing is both dangerous and shows a lack of regard for me – not only as your father but also as your captain." His lined face grew more serious, as his bushy eyebrows clung together. "You know that I will need to punish you for what you did, Eleanor. As much as it pains me to do this, you are to be confined to your quarters for two days."

"Two days?" Eleanor gasped, staring at her father. "But I will miss the exploration!"

Her father nodded gravely. "I have to show the crew that I am not afraid to punish you, even though you are my daughter." A hint of a smile pulled up the corner of his lips. "Just be glad it is not the cat o'nine tails, Eleanor."

Eleanor sagged against the chair, her ladylike position gone in a moment. Reflecting on her father's decision, she had to admit that it was fair, lenient even. She hated that her impulsive nature had, once again, brought severe consequences. If only she had not dived into the water to see what it was that glistened below! If she had only told her father, then he would have dropped the anchor and sent someone down – although Eleanor doubted that he would have chosen her. Even though she could swim like a fish, her father always kept her in his sights whenever he could.

"I am sorry you will miss the exploration of the Blackmoor Caves," her father continued, gently. "But Eleanor, you must know that you cannot simply do what you please on this ship."

"I do know, Papa," Eleanor replied, dully, ashamed that her the whole ordeal caused her to feel like a child when she would prefer to be treated as the sailor she was. She could only hope the treasure would yield results that would make all forget about the find and focus on the outcome. "I'm sorry."

Her father placed a gentle hand on her shoulder, getting to his feet. "Like you say, however, we have retrieved three trunks."

Hope sparked in Eleanor's chest. "You mean, I can open them?"

He chuckled. "I think so. After all, you were the one who spotted the locks gleaming under the ocean's waves."

Eleanor rose, her booted feet clattering across the wooden floor of the cabin as she made her way towards the trunks. She would have to change into dry clothing, but that could wait. "It is only because we are in such shallow waters," she said, bending down to examine the trunks. "Had the water been any deeper, then I doubt we would have found them."

"Here." Her father handed her a large mallet, and, using all her strength, Eleanor hit the lock.

It broke easily, evidently having been underwater for some time. With bated breath, Eleanor pushed the top of the trunk back. A wide grin spread across her face as she took in the bounty.

"There is some gold here," she cried, pulling out a gold coin and handing it to her father. "Not much, but enough."

Chuckling, her father picked up the mallet and broke the other two locks, finding more gold and some silver in the other two trunks. He crowed with delight as he grasped great handfuls of coins, letting them trickle back down into the trunk. Despite her impending punishment, Eleanor could not help but smile too, delighted that they would have more than enough to pay the crew for the next quarter.

"Everyone shall have a bonus!" her father declared, getting to his feet and throwing open the door to his cabin. "Morgan!"

The first mate came stumbling in, as though he'd been waiting for the captain to call his name. "Aye, Captain Adams?"

Eleanor grinned as her father slapped Morgan on the back, before gesturing towards the treasure.

"Here," he said. "Sort this out. Crew's pay and a bonus for everyone. Leave the remaining treasure in the first trunk."

Morgan returned Eleanor's smile, and got to the task at once, jubilant over some of the wonders he was finding. It would take him an age to sort out the treasure into piles of equal worth, but Eleanor knew it was a job the first mate thoroughly enjoyed.

Wiping down her breeches, Eleanor got to her feet and smiled at her father, wondering if he might forget her punishment.

Unfortunately, he had not.

"Right, Eleanor, to your cabin. Your meals will be sent down."

A sigh left her lips as she trudged past him, sniffing inelegantly. Behind her, she heard her father chuckle.

"Two days will be over before you know it, my dear," he said, following her out. "And if we find anything at the caves, you may join in the salvaging."

That was a slight relief, making her shoulders rise from their slumped position. "Thank you, Papa," she mumbled, as the fresh air hit her lungs. Taking in another few breaths, Eleanor took in the smell of the sea, the wind whipping at her hair....before she realized that the entire crew was watching her.

Taking a breath, she lifted her chin. "I should not have dived off the boat without alerting someone to what I had found," she said, loudly. "I did you all wrong by acting so impulsively and showed disrespect to our captain. I will not do such a thing again." She caught the look of sympathy in some of the crew's eyes, although they appeared to be relieved that she was receiving some kind of punishment. Without another word, Eleanor turned on her heel and walked down the short staircase to her cabin below.

Being the only woman meant she had one of only two tiny cabins below deck – Morgan, the first mate, held the other. Pulling open the door, she looked glumly into her gloomy room, hating that she would be stuck inside for two days.

"Thank you for your apology, Eleanor," her father said, holding the door as she walked inside. "The crew respects you, as they do me. They will hold you in greater esteem because you have confessed your wrongs."

Eleanor tried to smile, sitting down heavily on the wooden bed. "Thank you, Papa. I believe the treasure I found for them may also have increased their sense of 'esteem' in me."

He grinned at her. "You're a pirate's daughter, Eleanor. Some might think that means we have no standards, no way of keeping control, but you know how precarious the sea – and the crew – can be. They are loyal to me, and I want them to be loyal to you too. One day, this boat might be yours." With a quick smile, he closed the door and left her to her thoughts.

Eleanor stared at the door, her father's words echoing around her mind. One day, she might have control of the ship? Be the captain? Could such a thing truly happen?

Eleanor knew that in the Navy, there would be no thought of having a female captain, but they were far removed from the Navy! Pirates did things differently and, if her father thought the crew would respect her as captain, then she would gladly step into the role, though she hoped it would be some time before her father gave it up and retired from the seas.

To be a pirate captain! The thought made her smile, despite her current situation. To roam the seas with her crew, searching for bounty and, in their case, helping those less fortunate. She could not think of a better life.

Quest of Honor is now available for purchase on Amazon and to read free in Kindle Unlimited!

MORE FROM ELLIE ST. CLAIR

Sign-up for the email list and get a free Regency Romance "Unmasking a Duke" sent straight to your inbox.
You will also receive links to free promos, limited time sales, and the newest reads by up-and-coming authors. You will also have an opportunity to join our "street team" and get regular advanced reader copies of books.

SIGN-UP HERE:

www.prairielilypress.com/ellies-newsletter/

ABOUT THE AUTHOR

Ellie has always loved reading, writing, and history. For many years she has written short stories, non-fiction, and has worked on her true love and passion -- romance novels.

In every era there is the chance for romance, and Ellie enjoys exploring many different time periods, cultures, and geographic locations. No matter when or where, love can always prevail. She has a particular soft spot for the bad boys of history, and loves a strong heroine in her stories.

She enjoys walks under the stars with her own prince charming, as well as spending time at the lake with her children, and running with her Husky/Border Collie cross.

facebook.com/elliestclairauthor
twitter.com/ellie_stclair
instagram.com/elliestclairauthor
amazon.com/author/elliestclair
goodreads.com/elliestclair
bookbub.com/authors/elliest.clair
pinterest.com/elliestclair

ALSO BY ELLIE ST. CLAIR

Standalone

Unmasking a Duke

Happily Ever After

The Duke She Wished For

Someday Her Duke Will Come

Once Upon a Duke's Dream

He's a Duke, But I Love Him

Loved by the Viscount

Searching Hearts

Quest of Honor

Clue of Affection

Hearts of Trust

Hope of Romance